The Malthouse

Dick Wingate

Published by **Book Empire**

Printed by Book Empire
www.bookempire.co.uk
Unit 7, Lotherton Way, Garforth, Leeds, LS25 2JY

Printed in Great Britain

ISBN 978-191-33-193-04

This is a debut novel by Dick Wingate who spent nearly fifty years in the town planning profession including ten years as a private consultant.

He was born and spent his first thirty years in Suffolk, and now lives in Norfolk with his wife, Maggie. They have four daughters, ten grandchildren and three great-grandchildren.

Dick is hugely grateful to Jenny and her colleagues at Book Empire for constant encouragement and helpfulness, and to his wife, Maggie for her patience and help in the initial proof-reading. Further thanks go to Nicky Lain and to Charles Passant for further suggestions for this 2nd edition.

This book is dedicated to old colleagues and to those who continue to battle away at the coalface of an ever-increasingly complex business.

October 2020

The Malthouse

APRIL

PROLOGUE

Jim Prentice couldn't sleep. It was a warm and sticky night for April, and his wife, Hazel was in the hospice with terminal cancer. He got up, went down stairs, made a cup of Horlicks and sat at the kitchen table with his mind in a whirl.

He had spent months wondering what the hell was wrong with her. She had hardly ever spoken with him, and certainly hadn't mentioned illness. He supposed that the pressure in his work at school, the work on the District Council, and the struggle with teenaged children had made him less tolerant and less understanding. Philippa wasn't so bad, but she hadn't really got to the teenage tantrum phase yet. Zac on the other hand, was being a nightmare. He was disruptive at school, and there were real signs that the drug menace in the town was affecting him.

He felt that the current situation was not tenable anymore, something had to give. It would be no good trying to talk it out with her, she wasn't able to understand, and it certainly would be fair to her to say anything now.

It's not as though he had let the Party down, although that was always at the back of his mind, but more a case of not knowing where he was or where the future was going to take him. Money wasn't the major problem, although his teacher's salary wasn't that bad, but the kids were always a worry.

Jim wasn't into fun anymore. In fact, he wasn't fun at all. The way that Government had drained resources from schools, with parents having to provide basic materials to help each school gain the sort of ratings that would ensure that central funds would still be there, all made him fume.

With Hazel so near the end of her life, he would have to seek out someone to talk with about his problems. Maybe living in the village was the problem. Were people talking? Was he being paranoid? He definitely needed some independent thought.

Tomorrow was another day, maybe he could focus on that.

An hour or so later Len Pollox was woken by a sheet of lightning and a massive clap of thunder. It brought back memories of a storm when he holidayed with Cass, his wife of 40 years on the shores of Lake Como.

He turned to see the emptiness of that side of the bed. It had been four years since they had slept together and that it had taken experts the last two to diagnose her with motor neurone disease.

During those latter years, she had become incapable of giving Len the home comforts he felt he deserved, and Cass' friend Janet Sweet had provided the necessary support in the house.

Rumours were rife, but Len was a tough old bird with his 67 years of battling had seen to that. He had seen action in the Navy, fought in the inter-services boxing tournaments where he traded blows, always with the expectation of winning.

That was Len. Never knew when he was beaten, ready for a scrap of any sort, but fighting for Cass' health provided one of his few losses.

Short and stocky, no more than five foot three, but a

solid twelve stone, the years had added some flab where once was solid muscle, and had taken their toll in the hirsute department. The head was polished, the nose becoming more prominent, and remnants of those early fights made the broken nature of the nose more noticeable and the cauliflower left ear where his defence had occasionally let him down to scything right hooks protruded more than ever.

Not a pretty sight then, but this never bothered him, and he led his troops in his own style. The local Labour Party had been his focus, it seemed forever, although he did have a pot-shot at standing for Parliament in a spectacular, but not unexpected defeat. This was a forever Tory county with the odd pockets where the Party held its own in the urban areas on the odd occasion.

He reflected that the fact that he had gained control in this District nearly four years ago, largely through a lousy performance of the Tories at national level. This had been a bit of a bonus for him, but he was aware of the narrowness of his majority.

It was only a few weeks before the next election, and he was desperate to retain control.

That bloody enquiry was coming up soon and he wasn't looking forward to it.

And, he had become close to wondering if his project at the Maltings would ever come off.

Tossing and turning in his bed, he went to his normal trick of saying "sod it", rolled over and fell asleep.

In the morning, as usual, Avril Danes rose at 6.30 leaving husband Jake snoring away, showered and prepared for another day in the local press office. Standing just five foot two in her tights she tied her black hair into pony tail and stared into the mirror where her pale blue eyes stared back.

No make-up today, nothing special on the agenda.

She took the stairs in her dressing gown and made a couple of rounds of toast, slapped on a pile of marmalade, boiled the kettle and made a mug of instant. The TV in the kitchen was brewing various bits of gossip when a "Breaking News" item told the world of a new strain of virus had been reported in Eastern Europe, and might be a difficult one to control. She remembered a talk by Bill Gates back in 2015 when he forecast that a major pandemic was almost certain in the next few years, crossed her fingers and hoped this wasn't to be another one. The Covid-19 back in 2020 was bad enough.

She piled her mug and plate into the dishwasher, and went upstairs where she woke Jake with his morning cup of tea and a Rich Tea biscuit, and put on her favourite jeans and black polo shirt.

She kissed Jake and reminded him to get the boys up soon and ready for school and college, knowing that the two with ADHD would want to follow their normal routine, and may take a bit longer to sort themselves out.

She let herself out and got into the new Crossland hybrid automatic, and drove the seven miles from her home in Hayle to the office in West Kenning.

Whilst she knew that every day was different, she wondered what was likely to spring a surprise today.

In Snetterbrook Hall, the Vice-Admiral polished his sturdy walking shoes, oiled his favourite walking cane and village and to its only shop, to get his copy of the Times as well as a packet of shag.

"Damned fine morning," he greeted Tariq, the shop owner and handed over one of his least favourite oily plastic five pound notes, telling Tariq to keep the change. He had thought of buying one of the magazines from the top shelf, but wasn't sure he could hide it from The Lady Hilda when he got home, so he forgot the idea, dreamt of the past, and strode back to the Hall.

"Not such a bad chap, after all, I suppose some of those foreign fellas are alright," he muttered to himself.

THE PREVIOUS SEPTEMBER

Chapter 1

It was one of those September days when the world seemed fresh and clear. The early morning cool was going to disappear and the sun would beat down over the Norfolk landscape. The landscape of heaths, of arable acres, of ancient woods, of waterways and a coast as good as anywhere on earth.

It was the sort of day that Dave Wakefield loved. He would take advantage of the light and take his camera out and be content just to have his eye on the compositions he would use for his love of painting. Big skies, big cliffs, albeit that they were eroding at an alarming rate, big flocks of waders, big fields with the occasional oak where once was a series of hedgerows, the myriad of churches with their round flint towers or wooden spires.

It was going to be a good day.

Dave had just enjoyed his sixtieth birthday with his wife Michelle and their four daughters, and yes, he had regrets that there had been no boys and that his family name would not continue into another generation, but that was a mere trifle to the love they all gave each other. It hadn't always been easy, and he remembered the teenage rants and squabbles, the worrying nights when one of them hadn't come home until the early hours, but, all in all they had turned out to be good people with good folk in their lives.

He had moved to Norfolk in the 80's after the turmoil of the reorganisation of Local Government ten years' earlier had unsettled many families, and he had moved north from Suffolk to take up a senior post in the Planning Department of the Parston District Council.

Now retired, Dave had been asked by friends and contacts, and by developers with whom he had dealt in the past, to put his experience into the world of gamekeeper turned poacher. As a consultant he worked the hours he wanted, turned down the work he didn't fancy, charged the big boys big money and helped out the individuals who had got themselves in trouble with the planners as best he could for little more than his expenses. The work had kept his mind working and had kept him out of Michelle's way. Above all it had given them the opportunity of good holidays, good cars and time to indulge their hobbies and their golf.

Today, he had risen early, kissed Michelle as she slept, and got into his new Hyundai Touson, camera and binoculars on the passenger seat, and drove north towards the coast, enjoying his Fleetwood Mac compilation on the media system and his granola bar.

The Norfolk market town of West Kenning has a history of heavy engineering and malting, the former having gone to the dogs in the 1970's and only a third of the malting buildings still in decent shape, with one of them still used as a satellite to those in other nearby towns producing top class malting barley for the brewing and distilling businesses that are thriving.

With a main part of employment in the handful of supermarkets and in the care homes of the town and nearby villages, the centre is overwhelmed with charity shops, pharmacies and estate agents. Similar to many, it certainly had its share of empty shops, a few banks, opticians, a couple of small hotels and the normal variety of pubs.

West Kenning sits within the Local District of Parston which is made up of towns, villages and open countryside. It is not the most affluent within the county. In fact some of the towns are characterised by areas of distinct neglect showing both the effects of the Government's austerity measures and lack of investment, unlike the tourist driven areas on the coast.

This was the District where Len Pollox was the political Leader. The Labour Leader.

As always, Len was up early, and got to work with his pads of paper and his old carpenter's pencil, and began by planning out his new project. This one would make money, he was sure. He needed to make a strong mark on the town to ensure that next year's elections went the right way for him. No going back to a Tory council where members looked after each other and their friends. This one was for the town as a whole. He would create a community centre with gym equipment, a decent lounge area with an affordable bar, committee rooms, dance stage and anything that he thought the town needed.

He would buy one of the old Maltings, and get his friend Mickey Grove to help him find the contacts he didn't have himself to make sure he got hold of it, and find the funds to make it successful.

Mickey Grove had grown up in and around the town and now lived in an old farmhouse four miles away on the edge of the village of Banganall.

Perhaps village is a bit strong, as it was more of a hamlet, but it still retained its little shop which doubled as post office and was run by a couple of old folk who had lived there all their lives. Now in their mid eighties but still active, they ran the place at a loss, but just wanted to carry on helping serve the villagers.

Big broad man was Mickey, forty eight years old, 6ft 3 and 17 stone, well muscled as expected of a builder and smallholder. He had a strong rural Norfolk accent, grew chickens in the summer and was getting his turkey stock under way ready for the profitable Christmas trade. In his main storage building he kept all his builders equipment, but much old pieces of kit spilled over onto the area beside the main drive.

His wife, Edna worked in one of the local supermarkets and keeps her money to herself, always thinking that there might be a day when she would want a different life. So far, she had not had the guts to get out of what was a difficult marriage. She didn't like some of the company that Mickey kept and knew that some of his dealings were more than a little dodgy. The rumours that spread amongst the supermarket staff were difficult to accept, but she kept her head down and her ears open.

She left Mickey to get his own breakfast, had her cereal and got into the old Ford Focus and drove to her early shift.

Mickey had made some money buying and repairing cottages and renting them out at crazy prices, mainly to second homers from the Home Counties. There was good money to be made and the tenants usually paid their way. Much of the work was not quite up to scratch, and Mickey found that he often had to return to the properties and do the necessary repairs. Edna had nagged him about taking short-cuts in his work, but the nagging had made no difference.

He was a rough and ready sort of man, in more ways than one.

He had built up a friendship and some form of trust with Len, and they had shared ideas on a number of occasions. This time Len wanted to use Mickey in his project and they arranged to meet in the next few days to sort out who was going to do what.

Chapter 2

Parston District Council has 49 councillors from across its wide acres, representing wards in towns and rural areas. The staff is headed by Bob Garner the Chief Executive, who manages the work in conjunction with Departmental Chief Officers whose tasks cover Housing, Environmental Health, Planning, Finance and Administration.

Chief Planner was Clive Painter, a short blond sixty year old widower with a pale moustache. He had been in the job for four years. Not the most forceful of characters but held his own with the councillors who were often after a bit of help for a constituent, or more likely a friend, in need.

Clive had one of those handshakes you could not forget. Vice-like it was, small hands but the history of his work in the front row of his rugby team showed what he meant. No anger in it, just a good firm shake.

His teams comprised the policy making team headed by Paul Rashford which concentrated on the preparation of the Local Plan for the District, monitoring how it was being implemented and any changes in legislation and national guidance, and then reviewing the Plan. Paul's team also dealt with the conservation of historic areas and buildings, and of the landscape.

The planning applications team was led by Jane Seabrook, and the building control team, that tried to ensure that new structures were safe, which was led by Brian Hastings. Looking after the administration was Audrey Forrester.

September was the time of the year when planners across the country were having to provide information about the state of their historic buildings, especially those on the "Buildings at Risk Register", as well as the state of the housing accommodation throughout their districts and boroughs.

At Parston the lead was taken by Henry Bonner, known as "HB" as he was the Historic Buildings Officer for the Council, and not "Hard Black". He was a biro man, and was sensitive to all things non-PC.

At 55, HB was an ex-hippy turned archaeologist turned expert in historic buildings. A woolly haired single man he lived his life in old jeans and long "sloppy Joe" jumpers, which he said was necessary when delving into the roof spaces of old Tudor buildings.

The number of buildings that needed to be in his report wasn't that large, and the ownerships and the type of buildings were very varied.

There were old war-time buildings going to rot, a few churches that could make great community facilities, windmills, some of which over the years had been fully repaired by a local Trust, but many more that needed lots of "TLC". Then there were a number of Victorian industrial buildings, including some previously used for malting barley, but now no longer used, abandoned, with slates slipping off the roofs, water getting into the timbers, rainwater drains leaking and overflowing so that the earth bases of the foundations were washed away creating huge cracks in the brickwork.

Ownerships were always an issue, with some private owners with no money to speak of and no buyers prepared to take the buildings off their hands, public departments who retained old housing stock but didn't use them, a couple from the Middle East and from the racing fraternity who spent too much on the finer things in life but didn't look after some of their own property, and the occasional Peer of the realm who, it seemed, couldn't "give a stuff".

All had to be contacted and attempts made to help them find solutions.

HB went through all his lists, and also through his little black book which never left his side wherein were many jottings of things he had seen on his travels around the District. So, a few more to add this year that weren't on the list last year, and he knew that some of the ownerships were a bit tasty.

Better talk to the boss.

Clive had an architectural background and was a talented draughtsman and artist, and the issue of historic buildings always held his fascination. HB was in favour and his work usually supported.

"Morning, Henry" said Clive as HB knocked and entered Clive's office clutching his set of files.

"Clive, how are you today? I must say we've got a few interesting ones here, and I need your final guidance before I start my report for the Committee"

"I'm good, thanks. Fancy a coffee?"

"No, thanks I'm fine. Got a jug of water on my desk. Better for me!"

"Right, let's get on, I've a briefing with the Chairman in an hour. Take a seat by the conference table and let's have a look at what you've got."

"Bit tricky some of these, Clive, as we have the usual suspects and a few new ones as well as the usual rumour mill. I'll deal with the ones that are always on the list and run through an update. Won't take long."

HB was right. The usual problem buildings were still unresolved, and while this was frustrating, those particular buildings weren't in really bad order.

"However, these two have owners where I think either you or the Chairman might be better taking up the conversation with them. Might add a bit more weight to the issue."

"OK, I'll chat with Tom and see what he says, although I can see the politics of this one being tricky."

"Before I go, Clive, there are a couple of issues I'm hearing about that could be very difficult. One is that some of these old buildings are used by addicts. Old Toby Bunch the local bobby has been called out on a number of occasions and social services have been brought in to see what we can do."

"Not, surprising, that," said Clive, "but it might put more pressure on us to see what powers we can use that might really help. Maybe I'll chat with Terry Whitefoot and see what he advises. What's the other one?"

"Well, I gather there is a rumour going the rounds, and Jane has heard it too, that the Leader is looking into the conversion of one of the Maltings. But I'm afraid that his track record gives little confidence. If there is truth in the story, it will be a tricky one for you to handle!"

"Yes, I take the point. Thanks for the update. I will take a few minutes of my briefing with the Chairman to see what his point of view will be. Talk to you tomorrow."

Two days later and after dark, a large dark blue BMW coupe drove into town and the driver got out, and walked to the normal meeting point.

"Leppo" was a shaven headed six foot of black muscle, down from London to supply his troops. Loads of weed but mainly heroin as well as some crack cocaine, and he wanted to see the guys who were his middle men and deliverers to the main users. The network was well established and the hard core of users were desperate to get their fill.

The kids were mainly in the late teens, some dropouts from school, some homeless, but all with the menace of mental problems, either from a tough regime of parenting or from traumatising bullying. Then there were those who merely got dragged into the group by being mates with someone in real trouble.

Zac Prentice was one of these.

Chapter 3

Clive had driven his Volvo to his Chairman, Tom's house twenty miles south in the flat landscape where the heathland and scots pines set the tone. The A11 thrust its way towards London across the heath and the sound of traffic was non-stop. Fighter jets from nearby RAF and American air bases made terrifying noises, rupturing the peace.

Tom Middleton and his wife Irene lived in a former farmhouse on the edge of East Bartham, surrounded by the sandy soil which was excellent for carrots and for the nesting of the rare stone curlew.

There was a pair of binoculars on the window sill and a shotgun in the locked cupboard for his few invitations to an autumn shoot.

Despite the country squire appearance, Tom was Labour through and through.

"Always look after the little man, old boy, "was his mantra.

He had been Chairman of the Planning Committee since the Party took control of the Council, and Clive had built up a trusting relationship with him.

"Good to see you again, Tom" said Clive and accepted the invitation to sit in the deep leather armchair that Tom indicated.

"Tea or coffee, Clive?" asked Tom, to which Clive went for the tea that he guessed would be Earl Grey.

"Irene! Clive's here, would you make some tea, dear, please?"

Irene popped her head round the door, told Clive not to get up, asked after his family, and left to prepare the drink.

"So, what's new?" asked Tom.

"We are getting ready to publish a report on the state of our historic and empty buildings. Usual annual report, but there are a few awkward matters that we need your advice on before we go too far"

Clive set out the problems and Tom accepted the task of smooth talking to the owners which needed that approach.

When Clive mentioned the rumour of Len Pollox's involvement in a possible shady deal, Tom shuffled in his chair, took a deep breath and merely said "Bugger."

"Think I had better talk with Jim. Perhaps I'll sleep on it first, though"

"Might be wise, Tom" said Clive as he accepted his tea and a chocolate Hobnob from Irene.

They chewed the fat for another half hour, with Clive updating Tom on the normal affairs of the Department, items that would be coming up at the next Committee meeting, and going through the growing workload of his team that were struggling with meeting the targets that the Committee had agreed.

"The real problem," said Clive "is that the Government are also setting tight targets, the regulations are becoming more demanding, and to tell you the truth, we need more manpower if we are to keep up, and to ensure no one goes under with some sort of breakdown.

 It's a good team we have here, and I don't want to be responsible for damages to anyone's health.

 It's either we review the staffing requirement or we have to decide what we cannot do.

I can prepare a report for you that we could chat through, and I will need to talk with the Management Team about the problems. I have to say that there are those around that table that will take some convincing, so I may need your help, if we find an agreeable way forward" "I feared we might be heading this way" said Tom, "Jim tells me that the troops are not happy bunnies at the moment"

Tom had given his Vice-Chairman, Jim Prentice the task of keeping close to the team leaders, and Jim was rumoured to be quite close to Jane Seabrook.

Jane was the head of the team that dealt with all planning applications. She was thirty eight with hazel brown eyes and chestnut dark hair that waved below her shoulders, five feet eight, slim with a good figure and neat ankles. She had one of those dimples in her chin that drew your eyes straight to her face. With a ready smile and a strong temperament she was able to say "no" whilst not looking uncomfortable about it.

Divorced with two teen-aged daughters she lived a life on the edge of West Kenning, a life which was full of frustration, work-wise, family-wise and sexually-wise. Born in Nottingham she went to the local University to gain her degrees that gave her entry into the world of town planning.

She loved the problem solving, the networking with other professionals, the banter in the office, and even the drudge of report writing gave satisfaction, but the constant grind of the sausage machine trying to clear her team's work, having to dole out the occasional bollocking, the annual assessments of her team's performance and the perpetual uncertainty of whether the councillors would make consistent decisions, all gave her head the sensation of having a food mixer whirling around in it.

Jane had got to know the patch better than anyone. Others had their areas to deal with, but she found it hard to find the time to get out of the office and see what was going on out there.

Today was a good day, the weather fine, and she had no meetings to attend. Her girls Molly and Lou were off to school and she wanted to check on a couple of developments where neighbours had been causing a bit of a fuss.

A quick bowl of yoghurt and banana, a clean of the teeth, last minute trip to the loo, and she was outside and getting into the Kuga when she spotted someone sitting in a car on the opposite of the road. "That's weird" she thought, "not seen anyone doing that before", and she drove off towards the south of the District, but turned back to check on that car. It was no longer there, and she was sufficiently concerned that she abandoned her journey for that day and went into the office.

Back in the Planning Office, a few days later, Clive managed to fix a meeting with Terry Whitefoot, the Council's senior solicitor. Terry was, on the face of it, a pale sort of a man. Prematurely grey, thin and wearing his pale grey suit with a pale blue tie he looked almost ghostly. Despite all that he was a very wise bird. Whilst his legal knowledge was obviously good, it was his tactical abilities that particularly drew Clive to really enjoy discussions with him.

"How are you doing, Terry," asked Clive as he entered the lawyer's office which accommodated the usual library of legal decisions, encyclopaedias and legislation, and a desk where half a dozen photographs of Terry's family adorned one corner.

"I'm fine, thanks, Clive. Fancy a coffee?"

"Just had one thanks, but a glass of water would be fine."

Terry buzzed his secretary and ordered the water, and moved to his small conference table, moved a box of files along the floor, and motioned Clive to one of the chairs.

"So, what's up, Clive?"

"Funny one, this. We are going through the state of the historic buildings, and I had a meeting with Henry the other day, when he put me up to the fact that a couple of the buildings were being used by druggies. The police have been informed, as well as Social Services, and there was a chance that the Council might get dragged into the issue."

"The other one is potential trouble. I gather that the Leader is up to his tricks again and is likely to promote his own private scheme for the conversion of one of the Maltings. Knowing how he has pushed the boundaries of "conflict of interest" in the past, we thought you should know"

"I have told Tom, who swore, but still said he would talk with Jim before he took the bull by the horns."

"Ouch," said Terry, "that is a good one to get the juices flowing. I'll let Bob know."

Chapter 4

Len Pollox was on the phone talking to one of the local architectural technicians who knew a bit about the planning system, but was renowned for taking instructions from desperate people who had little chance of getting their plans passed.

Len had been known to lend his weight to some of these schemes, and, by leaning on some of his weaker labour colleagues who sat on the Planning Committee, he had not been surprised when the approvals were achieved.

Not for the first time this more than irritated Jane and her team, although Clive had told them that "this was the price of democracy".

"What's the sense of getting the Committee to agree a set of policies and then go completely against them?" queried Jason Quail, one of the younger members of her group. "Fucking crazy. What the hell are we supposed to say to the next dodgy proposal?"

"Jason, as time goes by you will experience many strange decisions which, you never know, might just provide the meat for a half decent novel! I know your writing style would be perfect for it," said Jane.

"Thanks, Jane, but do you see the frustration in many of us?"

"Yes, of course I do, I feel the same, but in this country of free speech and acceptance of everyone's right to think the way they choose, we will always see decisions we don't like.

"I know, but when they have agreed that something should be done one way, and then go and agree something that is a different way, it makes no sense. It's hypocrisy, and I think it's probably corrupt."

"Jason, it is great that you see this so clearly, but the world goes round on unacceptable decisions, and it's not something we can control. It is the system we have. Accept that, or you will go crazy with your frustration."

"Well, fuck it, I say," said Jason and grumped off to get a cup of coffee, mumbling about butchers, bakers and candlestick makers.

Meanwhile Clive was debriefing HB following his meeting with Tom, and they agreed to meet again in a week or two.

Mickey Grove had tracked down the mobile number for Leppo and asked if he would help to fund something good for the town, to offset the problems that his drug business was causing, and to usefully use money he was making out of "the poor sods you've got on the hook."

Mickey didn't mind the odd spliff himself but the heavy stuff was too much for him.

Leppo said he'd think about it, but wanted to know how much they were talking about, and spluttered a "no way, man" when he was told they were looking for a million or two.

Jane was enjoying her promised ride out in the September sun, the hedge lined roads and the views across the fields of harvested barley brought her mind back to the issue of the old malting and the rumours around Pollox's way of doing business.

"Whilst he may not be possible to stop, it maybe that there could be a way of making life uncomfortable for him," she thought.

She also had in mind the problems at home with the girls. Molly, the elder of the two was in the midst of a fortnight of angst, and typical teenageism.

Nothing was right. Everything Jane said was wrong and was out to stop her doing what she wanted. Why couldn't she go to the rave on Friday night? She was seventeen, after all. Jane knew that she was well developed and was liked by her friends at school, especially the boys.

Jane was scared. There was no man in her life who she could share these problems with and she didn't want to bother her parents who still live in Nottingham. She knew her mum would only hark back to her own teenage years and the pressure she was under, the wreck that was her bedroom, the TV on whilst she attempted to do her homework which had irritated her dad and had led to raised voices.

Her ex, John, lived away from the town but not that far away, and she decided to see if he was at home.

Their divorce had been a messy one, but they had tried to retain some form of communication for the sake of the girls. John had the girls for the odd weekends, and they were fond of his company.

"Mum's for the boys, dads for the girls" she mused.

Len put down his phone and shuffled some papers he - needed for the next meeting of the Council where he was having to defend his lack of action in the development of social housing that had been a major plank of his early speeches. He really ought to talk to his "cabinet" of committee chairmen, but he was known for blundering on in his own sweet way.

Many called it Trumpism.

He rose from his chair and went to make a coffee when the phone rang.

It was Mickey.

"Hiya Len, I've had a thought about the malting thing you were on about. I know it's a bit dodgy, but there's a guy who is rolling in it and may be able to provide funds."

"Bit busy at the moment, Mickey. Got a shed load in my diary and some awkward questions coming at me soon. I need to prepare my counter attack. I'll call you back in a couple of days".

Twenty minutes later, Jane drove up to John's house expecting him to be at work, but hoping otherwise. She rang the bell and waited a couple of minutes before she heard footsteps coming to the door.

She was met by a pretty blonde woman in a bra-less tee-shirt, who must have been ten years younger than her, and guessed this was John's new plaything. She introduced herself and asked if John was at home only to see him coming down the stairs and adjusting his trousers.

"I'm Belle" said the blonde.

"I bet you are" thought Jane, but kept a tight lip.

"Ah, John. I was passing through the village to see the site of a scheme that was causing the neighbours some grief, and just wanted a word about Molly. I know you are supposed to see the girls this weekend, and would be grateful if you can wheedle out of her what is going on in her mind. Is it just teenage stuff, or is there a problem? No real inquisition but a gentle word, please. Let me know how it goes"

"Yes, sure" said John taking a sideways look at Belle, "I suspect it's just her age, but I'll see what I can find. Thanks for popping by."

With that Jane turned and strode back to the car.

"Bastard," she mumbled "Yet another bimbo. Too much fucking testosterone in his pants"

Her mood worsening, she decided that, despite the intended site viewing, she would go home and work there, where at least she could open a new bottle of Pinot Grigio.

At least, that wouldn't wind her up.

Come the weekend, John decided he had other things to do, and let the girls down.

Not for the first time.

OCTOBER

Chapter 5

It was almost an Indian summer.

It was the sort of day when the very early mist would be burnt off very quickly and the sun would beat down onto a happy world.

Avril Danes rose at 6.30, and as usual left husband Jake sleeping, showered and prepared for another day in the press office.

She took the stairs as she wrapped around her dressing gown and chose cereal for breakfast, boiled the kettle and made her normal mug of instant coffee. She put her mug and bowl into the dishwasher, and went upstairs where, as usual, she woke Jake. She told him that it might be a long day, dressed in black slacks and a red blouse, kissed him goodbye and left for the office.

She always thought that each day would be different, and had a funny feeling that this one would be unusual.

As soon as she was at her desk, the phone rang and a voice she didn't recognise merely said "The Malthouse and the Leader" and rang off.

She had hardly got her head round this, when her new recruit came in with a leather man-bag across his shoulders and a smile on his young face. Geoff Pulling was just out of University, and at twenty-two was looking for a good, long career in journalism. He was a fresh faced man of medium build, with thick curly hair and black rimmed spectacles.

Avril had warmed to him at the interview and felt that he would be relatively easy going, but a bit of a rottweiler when it came to winkling out stories which the local readership would suck up. That sort of reputation would do him well in the future, but he had to tread very carefully, and she had warned him that some of the locals were a bit spiky, whilst, with a smile he would charm the majority.

"Morning, Geoff, any hangover today?"

"Fresh and fit as a fiddle today, Avril, thanks"

"You heard anything about the old malting buildings?"

"Well, I overheard someone in the pub the other night, saying that there were a lot of drug problems there. Do you want me to see if I can ferret anything else out?"

"I'm not sure there is anything in it, but just keep an ear out."

Avril went back to her laptop, browsing the local social media groups to see if there were any tasty titbits that might lead to a decent story.

Len was getting unusually edgy, and rang Mickey to see if there was any further progress from his end of things.

"Last time you rang you hinted that there might be a way of getting the funding for the project, but you hinted it might be dodgy," he said.

"I've had a word with a few of my people and the word is that the normal bunch with a bit of loose cash aren't flush at the moment. As you know there's all this drug money floating around, and I think I can get you a meeting with the local "King of the Streets" if that would help. It might be where you could get your money from." replied Mickey.

"That won't look good, Mickey, unless we can keep it well under wraps"

"I know, mate, but I'll see what more I can find out. See ya."

With that Len put the phone down and rubbed his forehead as if to loosen up his head muscles.

Looking towards the future, he then gave some thought to how he might get support from his Labour colleagues, who he could count on, and who he was pretty sure would be against him.

He was aware that over the last three years or so there were those whom he had alienated, and he went through the list and put a tick beside the names of those who were the cast iron "with-him" people. There were those that he knew he had some dirt on and who might not want to stray too far from his fold too.

"Do I have enough control?" he wondered.

He was also mulling the fact that in six months he would be fighting to keep the Party in control, when the elections took place in May. It wouldn't be long before people would be agitating to be on the lists for candidature for the various wards in the District.

He might test out Tom Middleton and Jim Prentice as the Planning Chairman and Vice-chairman.

"Hmmm, I'd better think long and hard," he mused.

Jim Prentice was enjoying an evening digging over his vegetable patch and looking forward to the football on the tele later.

He was struggling with his job as at the town's Westgate High School, and with the problems at home, where the kids Zac and Philippa were constantly playing up and his wife, Hazel was less than comforting. He suspected that Zac, the elder of the two, might be meeting up in bad company but there was no proof, and neither of them was in a frame of mind to address the issue.

Jim was 45, good mid-life crisis material, and his brown hair was thinning rapidly. He had been a Labour supporter for twenty-odd years, was now a "sports jacket with leather elbows" man and taught geography at school. The enthusiasm for the subject had led him to the fringes of the planning issues, and he had pushed himself into seeking the Chairmanship of the Planning Committee once the Party gained control those three and a half years' ago. In the end he was disappointed when Tom Middleton was chosen, but accepted the role of Vice-Chairman. He got on well with Tom and they forged a useful partnership as well as a working friendship.

He enjoyed the fact that two of the Town Councils in the District were in Labour control and knew most of those members. The population of the District was split equally between those who lived in the towns and those in rural locations, so that there was a considerable variation on the demands placed upon the Council.

He had chosen to live in the village of Swinton, just outside West Kenning which afforded him a bit of time each morning to enjoy the countryside as he drove the second hand Subaru Forester into work. It was the perfect car for his site visits throughout the countryside with the Planning Committee which were sometimes needed to understand the issues surrounding some more difficult applications.

He enjoyed living in a vibrant village where there was a couple of local shops, particularly an excellent butcher, a couple of pubs and a reasonable bus service.

His mind also wandered to other things.

At Snetterbrook Hall on the edge of the village of Easthoe on the south side of the A11, Vice-Admiral Sir Douglas Ewart-Robinson was reaming his old briar pipe and looking out across the estate. He took a particular interest in local affairs and liked to inform the press and the authorities of that interest.

A slim, upright man of seventy two, with slicked back silver hair and big bushy black eyebrows, he kept himself in shape with daily vigorous walks around his grounds and along the disused railway track that ran beside the Hall.

Lady Hilda, his wife of forty five years was a prim little woman who preferred plaid skirts and twin-sets walked with him with quick little stuttering steps, and enjoyed her evenings of bridge with her lady friends, together with a few glasses of dry sherry.

Lady Hilda was also not shy in making her views known.

Back in the offices of the Broad Norfolk Post, Avril and Geoff were busy on the phones chatting to their usual contacts to see what might break as a decent story.

Little new was coming to the surface.

"Perhaps we'll have to invent something," said Geoff with a smirk.

"Never been done before," Avril grinned at him. "Oh, yes I know. Fake News. It depends on what you want to believe, doesn't it"

"Not round here, though," asserted Avril, "although there is always a first."

"I can see the editor loving that. I bet it would sell lots of papers, though!".

"Come on, Geoff, get off the fantasy planet, and get back down to earth. We've got to be real."

A few minutes passed and Avril's phone rang.

"Morning Boss, how's it going?" Avril said with more politeness that normal.

"Avril, I'd like you to look at local priorities," said the Editor, "what's the worst thing going on at the moment? How are the various authorities getting on with solving that? What is the political situation like when there are elections coming up in the next six months or so?"

"OK, it's certainly quiet at the moment. We'll put a list of issues together and come back to you."

Avril briefed Geoff and split the tasks between them.

"I'll focus on the political stuff, you have a poke around the others. I suspect the drug issue will be high on the list. Let's see if we can really nail down who's involved."

Chapter 6

Jane Seabrook was still fretting, even after her third glass of wine, and couldn't shake the problems with Molly out of her mind.

"Christ, she can't be in the club, can she? I've not seen too many signs of that. Not heard her throwing up in the mornings. No, it can't be that"

She poured her fourth glass and found there was little left in the bottle, so finished it off, and realised that she hadn't had any lunch yet.

"Perhaps she's had a falling out at school. Girls can be awful to each other," she thought, "maybe she's been bullied. Maybe she's got into the wrong crowd".

Pulling herself together, she made a thick ham sandwich with a good dollop of mustard in it, and settled down on the sofa to watch the news.

Within five minutes, she was asleep.

Len Pollox was on the move.

He got into his ten year old Mercedes 200 and went to the Council offices to meet up for his weekly discussions with the Chief Executive.

Bob Garner was a charismatic 45 year old who had been brought in by the previous Tory leadership to try and make the Council more effective, and to cut costs. He had previously worked in the motor industry and was full of ideas that many of the senior management found interesting, if sometimes a bit giddy. A big man with ginger hair, he was unusual in that he rarely lost his temper.

At least not in the office.

Needless to say, many of Len's Labour colleagues were unhappy with the tightening of the belts and the reduction of staff. Nevertheless they spoke freely to each other, and were able to disagree over a coffee and biscuits without too much rancour. It was the women who had no time for him.

Bob knew which side his bread was buttered and, whilst he might have a bit of fun by putting out some fancy ideas that he knew would go down badly, was well aware that the Councillors were the ones to set the policies and targets for the staff to try to implement and achieve.

After half an hour of Bob updating Len on the general issues of the previous few days, he asked the Leader what the general mood of his colleagues was like, and if there were any new initiatives that Len was wanting to promote, bearing in mind the elections in May.

"Apart from trying to sort out the drug taking problem, I've got one or two private projects that I'm thinking about, and will let you know when we need to get the approvals through."

Bob twitched a bit, thought for a minute and said "I really do think that you need to be very aware of the conflict of interest thing, and the effect not just on your reputation but, more importantly, on the Council as a whole."

"I don't need reminding of that, thank you," said Len with a grimace, "and I've had a lifetime of looking after myself."

"That's exactly what I mean," thought Bob, and realised the meeting was at an end as Len rose and turned towards the door.

Down at the Queen's Head, a few of the locals were enjoying a pint of Adnams, and passing the time with a game of cribbage or dominos.

"Heard the latest thing that old Len is up to?" asked one, to nobody in particular.

" Bound to be a lot of hot air and no action, whatever it is," came a half interested reply.

"What they need to do is sort out that bloody scruffy old building that the druggies use, then perhaps they'll bugger off," said a third, who looked as though he might be one of them.

Christian Grimm, a second-hand car dealer who owned a few poorly maintained flats in the town, had listened to all this, and couldn't make up his mind whether to get involved. He had been on the wrong end of a couple of schemes that Len had put to him, and didn't want to seem to be supporting him. However, he was aware of some good things that the man had done for the town, albeit that he may have feathered his nest at the same time.

Grimm was a tall, slightly bent over character with a good head of long hair that blew around in the breeze. He earned himself a decent wedge each month and enjoyed getting amongst the gossip, and mixed with some of the businessmen, always playing a bit above his station. He had owned a couple of shops in town, but when the tenants failed to pay their rents for a few months he just told them to get out. No thought of going to solicitors, no thought of going to the bank. He sold the shops and made a little on the deal. He had always enjoyed going around town in a flashy car since he was a boy-racer, and bought and sold a number of half decent cars, and he knew there was always the odd rough one that he had made good money on, but had let the owners down later. Christian knew a bit about *caveat emptor* – let the buyer beware, and could usually handle the odd unruly buyer.

He played a bit of golf, but spent most of his round doing deals over the phone. One of these deals would come good one day, he was sure. However, one thing that always went spectacularly wrong was his relationship with women.

This was down to his arrogant and misogynistic attitude. Christian made sure that he was always right.

Not always.

In the corner of the bar young Geoff Pulling was reading the Sun, whilst cocking an ear to the conversations. "Might come back here in a couple of days. Feels like something is cooking!" he thought as he finished his pint, and he went out into the street, put his phone to his ear and called Avril.

Chapter 7

Avril had been trying to find what was happening on the political front and thought that a chat with Jim Prentice might be profitable. He was an affable sort, and was reasonably close to the action.

That evening she rang Jim. "Sorry to bother you of an evening," she said, "but I wonder if we might have a general chat sometime so I can give the local readers an insight into the current planning problems – if any – and into the way you think the next six months will go, leading up to the elections."

Jim was receptive and they agreed to meet in a few days time.

Avril wanted something earlier than that, but was convinced that that it could wait, and satisfied herself by working on Geoff's report.

Local police sergeant Toby Bunch had indicated that "there is insufficient police staff to keep a constant watch over the town of West Kenning.

The local weekly edition of the paper included a short article:-

> ### Drugs and strange dealings - Rumours Denied
> *A number of folk in West Kenning have been talking about the use of the old malting buildings.*
>
> *It appears that one is the chosen centre of drug dealing, and we are aware that the local police force is active and trying to keep it under control.*

Local police sergeant Toby Bunch has indicated that "there is insufficient staff to keep a constant watch over the place, but we are gathering good information." The other talking point surrounds a scheme that the Labour Leader of the Council appears to be working on, and the reasons for doing so. So far, we have been unable to get his confirmation of this.

Molly Seabrook was late out of school, and made her way to the centre of town and joined the queue in Greggs for the sort of sweet bun she knew her mother would detest.

That and a full fat Coke and she was out of the door, wandering the streets with a few of her friends.

"Not sure if I'm going home tonight," she said to no one in particular, but Zac Prentice overheard and came up to her grinning from ear to ear.

"Watcha want, Zac?"

"Just a chat, see if you're OK"

"What are you really interested in, Knobhead"

"Steady on, I'm just trying to be friendly"

"Well, go and be friendly with someone else," she sulked.

"Look, if you don't want to go home, why not hang out with us?"

"Why, watcha doing, then? Off to that drug house?"

"Might be."

"What happens there...really?"

"Get a bit stoned. Have a laugh. Come on it'll be fun"

"Dunno, I'm in enough bother already. My head's in a real mess. 'Spose I ought to get home really."

And with that she turned on her flat heels and went to catch the bus to her home on the edge of town.

Jason Quail was getting up his usual head of steam about nothing very important. The workload in the Planning Department was building up unusually for this time of the year, and the paperwork and the need to check even more aspects of ordinary proposals was getting right up his nose.

He had entered the profession with the bright intentions of doing good for the community, but the general grind was doing nothing for his enthusiasm.

All the admin team seemed to do was make more work for him in checking that every process had been carried out properly, otherwise the bloody targets would get missed, another few boxes couldn't be ticked and the bloody ombudsman would be brought in again.

"I just need to get my teeth into a decent case so that I can show them I'm not as dozy as some of them think," he told himself, and left off and went to the pub.

Meanwhile Geoff Pulling was swiping his way through social media, the local groups, and the twitter feed from those in the town and the surrounding area.

For such a young cub reporter, he had a ready eye for the snippet that might get him in the really good books of the Editor.

One stood out and a couple of names caught his eye. "Mmm," he thought, "I wonder if "@Zacboy" might be worth a trace. Unusual name."

He checked the threads of discussions, and it seemed that he might be right.

He rang Avril with his thoughts.

When Molly got home, she found her mother kneeling in the bathroom with her head down the "big white telephone", making all sorts of foul noises.

"Oh, God, not again," she thought, and rather than going to her room with her hands over her ears, she did something out of recent character. She comforted Jane, cleaned her up and took her to her bedroom, where she loosened her mother's belt, undid the catch on her bra, and gently laid her down with her head resting on three pillows.

Molly had been ready for a reasonable chat with her mum, but that would have to wait.

She went to her room, plugged in the headphones to her mobile and listened to her favourite music.

She was getting fed up with Lady Gaga and Ed Sheeran, thought Sam Smith was a bit odd and that George Ezra didn't look like his voice sounded.

It was back to Little Mix and Harry Styles for her now, and Spotify was doing her proud.

After an hour of music, she went to see how Jane was, she touched her gently on the shoulder, fearing that she might have passed out, or worse, passed away, and she sighed with relief when Jane opened her eyes, looked quite bright and gave Molly a big hug.

"Must have been something I ate," she said, smiling at her daughter.

"More like that bottle of wine you drank," Molly replied. "How are you feeling? You really did look like a real wreck."

"Sorry, dear, I really am. I was near your Dad's house this morning and called in to see if he was OK to have you girls this weekend, only to find him with some slutty bimbo."

"Oh, she's OK. She's been living with him for a few months' now. They seem happy."

"Well, it really pissed me off, and I got into one of my moods and came home, and then "

"Alright, but you worried me, mum, and I do love you, and I know I've been a little shit lately, and I know I've not helped you when you're out at work making sure we live a half decent life. I know it's awkward for you with Dad, but I don't know how I can get this stuff in my head sorted out."

Jane looked her in the eye, and the dam burst. They both flooded tears and hugged longer than they could remember.

Molly's sister Jessica Louise, known as Lou was four years younger, and was a sickly child. Her condition was caused by a genetic problem affecting her breathing and gastric system. Years of visits to doctors and hospitals had given her a degree of stoicism, but she was, clearly struggling and missing a fair bit of school.

Jane and John's divorce had given both girls a lot of mental health problems as well, even though Jane had done her best covering up the real anger she felt towards their Dad.

Lou was in her room, doing what school work she could on her iPad. Jane then decided it was time to unburden herself to Molly.

"Look, Molly, I'm sorry I'm in such a state. My work is really stressful, I am constantly worrying about Lou, you are being a typical teenager with your hormones all over the place, and on top of it all your father is being a real shit."

"Oh, Mum," she said, giving her as big a hug as she could.

"I know, but he hasn't paid me what he should for child maintenance for months. He'd been seeing so many other women whilst we were married, and eventually I had to kick him out. At that point he said he'd make my life hell. And he has. I hate the bastard," and with that she sobbed the sobs of a child.

Hearing the noise, Lou entered the room, and asked what the matter was, only to be brought into the group hug.

Avril was ready to let the Editor know what she thought the main features in the local news should be, namely drugs, tatty buildings, empty shops, one or two bad private landlords. These were the main topics at the moment, together with the likelihood of a few controversial planning applications.

There might also be local conspiracy story, but that was only a rumour at the moment.

"So," she said, "we've split the work between politics and the tatty side of life."

"Aren't they the same?" chuckled the Editor.

NOVEMBER

Chapter 8

It was the first of the month and Clive Painter was in the office by seven thirty, ready for a day of updates on the progress of a series of policy documents he had requested, along with the issues concerning the historic buildings.

He would set aside the morning for these briefings with his staff, and then look to make the afternoon free to make sure that Tom and Jim were told as much as they needed to know.

The Committee still seemed to be behaving reasonably well; perhaps this was down to the way the Chairman and his Vice controlled things. He certainly hoped so.

HB was the first to arrive, still with his cycling Lycra clinging to his lithe body and went to the gent's room to change. He undid his back-pack and swore to himself as he realised he hadn't packed any new socks, so he'd have to either go sock-less to the meeting or wear his white and green cycling ones. He chose the latter to reduce the chance of blisters.

"Morning Clive," he said as he entered the boss' office, "good day for the race!"

"Morning Henry, how was the ride in today?"

"Yeh, it was a good one. A good work out. I'm ready for the fray!"

"Excellent, let's get down to it. What's new?"

"Well, apart from the normal ones, we've found a new case down in Dilford. Fiona James rang to tip me off about it. It seems that the old Listed Victorian ammunition store on the common has been vandalised, so I'm going to take a look at it later today. I'll go with "Jimmy" Young, as I didn't bring the car today."

Peter "Jimmy" Young was one of the planning enforcement team. An ex-copper who had played professional football in the lower leagues, and his experiences in the force had given him the perfect attitude for the job. He was a burly man, but quietly spoken until he got his dander up when he could be suitably forceful.

"Whilst you are with him," said Clive, "see what he knows about the drug den here. I bet he's spoken to Toby Bunch."

"Will do, but what's the latest from the top about the leader and his cronies?"

"It's certainly creasing a few brows," said Clive, "I think it will be a few days before we get any clarity on that one." "Have a good trip to the "deep south" this afternoon, and....Henry I love the socks!"

Clive was content with the progress so far, and was preparing for the briefing from his policy team led by Paul Rashford.

Five minutes later Paul knocked on the door and entered clutching his mug of coffee, together with Andrea Youngs, his assistant and Vijay Bhatt a newcomer to the team on a one year contract to help with the development of the Local Plan for the whole District. He was taking a year out of University to get some hands-on experience, and he was doing well.

"Morning all. Thanks for your time. I suggest we understand the current categories of your workload, and then look at the progress in each," said Clive, and there was general agreement to that approach.

Paul said, "Yes, that's fine, Clive. I suggest we work through the Local Plan, the Landscape Policy work, and I have asked Kirsty to join us for that, and of course, you have just had your session with HB."

"Yes, that went well. He's doing a good job."

"Thanks," said Paul. "As you know, the processes and requirements of the Plan have been messed about by Government recently, but we've managed to allow for those changes to be incorporated in our work. I've suggested that we set out the main criteria for the Plan, such as sustainable development, not just where we allow for housing and employment areas, but we also need to include matters like energy production, water supplies, traffic use. But how can we control it?

"We can only encourage, but we also have to show that we are not at the sharp end of proactive development and can't provide what is required – more's the pity!

"We will show how we can resist where there ar good reasons to do so, like the landscape, infrastructure, conservation etc., and we need a policy regarding enforcement of conditions imposed on planning permissions. Andrea is dealing with the housing issues, so I'll let her update you on that."

"Thanks Paul," said Andrea, "I have to say that we are struggling to get a grip on detail, in that we have already got loads of land with permissions that developers are sitting on and just not making any progress. So we don't know how many houses will eventually get built there, or what sizes they will be."

"But, there's nothing new there," said Clive, "We've always had to have a bit of a stab in the dark and work on the average numbers on sites already developed."

"Yes, but it would be great to be a bit more accurate in the estimates. For example, we know developers will want to maximise profit by building bigger three, four or even five bedroom homes, whereas the local demand is probably more geared to two and three bed houses and bungalows for youngsters, single people and older folk, and I know people are worried about where their grandchildren will live. If we do crack that one, we have to work out how much more land we need to allocate to accommodate the expected growth that Government and the County have agreed. People talk about the need for so many houses, but I wish it could be better related to the number of people. Again that ought to relate to the types of dwellings that folk need. It's all a bit "finger in the air", isn't it?"

"Always has been," said Clive.

"Then," continued Andrea, "there is, of course the matter of where do we allocate that required land. Do we go for a new village where we can make sure that all the necessary infrastructure will eventually be there to serve the residents, or do we go for a scattergun approach which won't provide land and funds for any new school, doctors, dentists etc.?" "How do we decide?"

"All good points, Andrea, thanks for that. Whilst we may well find a technical conclusion, it will have to be a political one in the end," replied Clive.

"We need to have a good look at the transport issues," said Paul, "We have to get the information to test how much additional traffic can be absorbed in each of the towns, how much will be too much especially in regard to road safety, air pollution, road capacity, and so on. How many cars would be generated by the new housing?

What about heavy vehicle increases to serve new employment areas, where would the increased number be travelling to? We need an expert survey and plan. The County may be able to do it, but I know there has been local criticism of them. Traffic consultants would definitely be independent, but expensive. What do we do, Clive?"

"I suggest you set all these questions into a report and we will ask the Committee how they want to proceed."

"OK, let's move on to the Landscape policy."

Andrea and Vijay left the meeting and went to tell Kirsty it was her turn.

Kirsty Abbott had a degree in Environmental Sciences and was hugely enthusiastic about her job, and churned out the work with great speed. Not that the spelling and grammar was always great, but the essence of her work was excellent. She had been the only person doing the work but was now recently joined by a French Student who was on a gap year, and was as bright as a button.

"Josie is helping out with collating the views of all the groups we have consulted. She has been with me when we met with the Environment Agency, the National Trust and the Wildlife Trust, and has been great coming up with some new ideas," said Kirsty. "I want us to have a completely joined up approach to this, and we are close to agreeing general principles, so that a draft should be ready within a month."

"How are you enjoying being here, Josie?" asked Clive. "Is this area very different from your home area?"

"It is very flat," she said, "my home is in the east of France, so there are lots of hills and mountains. But this is nice and it is a nice team to work with, for sure."

"Excellent, Josie, and you grasp of our language is very good. Well done," said Clive and thanked them for their work.

Kirsty and Josie left and Clive and Paul chewed the fat for a while, realising that very little was new in this business.

There was always a chance that they might be re-inventing a large wheel!

Chapter 9

Down in the expanded town of Dilford, where there were more council houses than private ones, the academic Labour councillor Fiona James was fretting over the fact that the bonfire on the common being prepared for the Guy Fawkes celebrations was looking larger than usual, and the proximity to the now vandalised old ammo store was a real threat to a part of the history of the town.

As a professor of Humanities at the University in Norwich, she had her principles, as well as her admirers. She was in her late forties, tall and well built with long dark wavy hair and almost black eyes. She had never married, but had enjoyed a number of partners of either sex.

As she waited for Henry Bonner to arrive, she scrolled through her phone to catch up on the local gossip.

HB and Jimmy were enjoying the chat on the way down to Dilford, and had spent twenty minutes talking about the football results and whether this team or that was likely to do what Man. City and Liverpool had done recently. It mattered little, but passed the time.

"Whilst we are talking competitions, what's the competition like in the local drugs scene? There seems to be more kids going about looking like bloody zombies."

"Well, according to Toby, the local force is trying to delve into it as gently as possible, and I suspect there will be some "busts" in the next week or so."

"Talking of busts, I guess Fiona will be getting worked up down there."

"What do you mean "down there", you dirty bugger!"

"Sod off, I meant that she'll be ready to give us the third degree!"

Fiona was standing by the ammo store when they arrived.

"Morning Henry," she greeted them.

"And a very good morning to you. Have you met Peter Young, our enforcement officer?"

"Oh yes, many times. This place always seems to keep you busy, doesn't it, Peter?"

"It has its fair share, but you are not alone, I can assure you!"

She looked around at the bonfire. "Since the bloody County started charging crazy money for the privilege of trying to recycle our waste, everywhere becomes a dumping ground, and I guess that's why this heap is so big this year."

"And it is a bit too close to the Listed Building," said HB, looking at the state of the structure.

It had been built of the traditional white bricks from the local clay, decorated with moulded dark red bricks around the doorway, and with a pitched roof of pin tiles. Inside was a concrete flat ceiling designed to protect the contents. The cast iron door was somewhat rusty and the keyhole clearly showed that there had been a big key needed to gain entry.

In truth, HB was surprised that there wasn't more damage to it. Paint spray used for graffiti, and what looked like pitted marks from air pistols, along with a few holes in the roof tiles, seemed to be the total effect of the vandals.

Despite the reputation of the place being a bit of a rough area to live, where the local gangs had been useful with their knives, there had been little evidence of "proper" weapons.

HB took a series of photos, and took a general look around the area while Jimmy was getting an earful from Fiona about a number of pretty trivial matters. At least, they seemed that way to him.

While Jimmy drove the car back to base, HB made a few notes on his phone, and emailed them to Clive.

They were back before lunch, and HB popped in to see if Clive was still at his desk.

Indeed he had just finished a session with the policy team who were in the latter throes of preparing a detailed strategy for the protection and enhancement of the landscape which had involved a lot of networking with environmental agencies and Trusts.

"Henry, thanks for the emailed notes. Nothing much there, then?"

"No, but the professor was mighty worked up about their bonfire structure!"

"Did you get into the old store? Could you see if there was anything still in there?"

"No chance; the cast iron door was well fixed, and I don't know who, if anyone, has the key. I'll try and talk to the Town Clerk and see if she knows anything."

"OK, Henry, but we need to get on with the overall report to the Committee, and hope they support all our recommendations!"

"Wonders would never cease," said Henry to himself.

Jim Prentice was thinking about the call he received from Avril, and wondered if the time was right to talk with the press. He could see if the chat would be "off the record", but still wasn't sure it was the right time.

His mind switched to Jane Seabrook and that fabulous body of hers. He couldn't believe that her husband would leave her for another woman, but he guessed these things happen. He knew his wife was becoming more distant by the week, and he couldn't remember the last time they had had a decent bit of rumpy pumpy.

He wasn't washed up yet, although she might be. Unless... "no she hasn't has she? She wouldn't, would she?" he thought.

Anyway, his mind was still undressing Mrs Seabrook, when his mobile rang.

It was Len wanting to hold a meeting of the Labour Group the following week.

"Fine with me, Len," he said, "what are the main talking points going to be?"

"Preparing for the election, and one or two other projects. I'll get an email sent."

Jim's mind was going back to the image of his favourite planner, but decided against it, and any call from Len would put any man off his stroke.

He would have to arrange to have coffee with her at some stage.

Chapter 10

Mickey Grove was in the back room of the Rat and Rabbit pub with his pint of Guinness half drunk, waiting for his meeting with Len. The pub was the scruffiest in town, wooden floors, plenty of dust, but Mickey liked its atmosphere. Not a load of loud music or too many youngsters. It suited him down to the ground. Time to think, time to drink.

Half an hour later Len arrived, and Mickey bought him a glass of cider and a packet of cheese and onion crisps.

"Evenin'."

"Mickey."

"This scheme of yours, tell me more about it, and what will be in it for me."

"All in good time, Mickey," said Len, pulling a folder out of his bag. It was one of Cass' old shopping bags and was the worse for wear.

"One thing I do know is that we're going to need a lot of money, and we have to find ways to get it."

"Need a specialist, Len."

They cost too much, and I'm not forking out for some fancy pants finance man to sort the matter out. I've done things before and I'll do them again."

"I know you have, but just remember some of the scrapes you got into. You're not some "Jack the Lad" nowadays, you have a position to hold up. Think about it, Len. Get yourself an accountant".

"Alright, smart-arse, what's your suggestion?" "Well, if you don't want to spend too much, why don't you see if Tubs Taylor can help? You know who I mean?"

"Want another pint, while we work this out?"

"No ta, I best get home, before my dinner is in the dog."

"Well, let me know if you have any other ideas."

"Night" And with that Mickey rose from his seat and went on his way home.

Len gave the matter more thought and decided that it might work out. But he didn't want too many people in the know until he had got the whole scheme clear in his mind.

In the morning he would ring Taylor.

In the early evening of the 5th, Fiona and many more gathered on the common in anticipation of the spectacular firework display.

At the stroke of 7 o'clock the organiser announced that they were ready to start the event, and hoped everyone would have an enjoyable and safe evening. Someone lit a flare and went round the base of the bonfire, lighting it every couple of feet. Someone else lit the first of the rockets which went up and ballooned into a globe of sparkling and crackling light.

The fire took no time to get going as more rockets of various sizes and heights lit the sky.

Parents were encouraging their kids to look up high, and the "Oooos and Aaahhhhs" brought the crowd to a height of enjoyment.

Hot dogs were eaten, beer and Cokes were drunk, and all seemed very well indeed.

And then...............

"Wooosh" "Bang" "Weeeeeeeeee", as the bonfire exploded, old gas canisters flying in all directions, flames going everywhere including into the box containing the fireworks, and all hell was let loose.

Despite the presence of a fire engine, the speed and ferocity of the explosion took everyone by surprise.

"There'll have to be a bloody enquiry into this," said Fiona as she shielded her hair from the raining sparks. "All that bloody rubbish dumped there, all because the County-bloody-Council was trying to screw the public with their costs to dump in the proper place."

Then, one of the pallets on the fire shot up into the air and landed on the roof of the ammunition store. HB would not be able to accept that vandals weren't at play this time.

Worst of all, the rockets were shooting off in all directions and the Town Mayor looked aghast as one of them shot straight at her youngest son.

The St John Ambulance had been stationed nearby, and the officers were in the vehicle keeping clear of the flying debris. They saw the boy fall and rushed to see him, blood all over his head and he seemed completely out of it. They tried to patch him up, but realised this was far worse than they expected, and called for the Air Ambulance which fortunately had started night flying in the last year.

The Mayor was being comforted by friends when another huge explosion took place and four huge Catherine Wheels rolled across the common towards the hot dog stand.

"Mustard, young man?" the owner said, looked up and squirted the contents over his partner before being enveloped in circles of fire.

Fiona, satisfied that all the emergency services had handles on the problems, walked away.

Filled with anger and sorrow that such a tragedy should happen in her town, she made her way towards home, when a couple of American airman from the local base tried to chat her up. Normally she might have tried her luck, but tonight she was in no mood and told them to "piss off."

She found the key to her door, crashed onto the sofa, thought about the disaster of the evening, rose, poured herself three fingers of Jameson Irish Whiskey which was drunk in two quick swallows, and went to bed.

Chapter 11

Next morning, Len looked up the number for Tubs Taylor and rang him.

"I need you to come and tell me how I can raise money for a community project." He said with his usual gruffness.

"I can make the afternoon of next Friday," said Tubs, sipping his weak cup of instant coffee.

"Too late, I need you tomorrow at the Labour Club at 1.45."

"Not sure, I can make it then. What's so urgent?" "I need you to tell me how I can raise funds for it. I need to brief my colleagues on Tuesday."

"Have you got a business plan? Any bank is going to have to go through that in some detail."

"Bugger that nonsense," said Len with growing frustration, "I just need names of those who can help me. If you won't, I'll find someone who will."

"That's fine, Mr Pollox, but you won't raise honest funds without a lot of hard work first. Even if you want to go the National Lottery, I can assure you that the process is no fun, and you will need a specialist to prepare your bid. Whatever you do, you will need a lot of upfront money before you even start work. And you'll need a planning consultant to guide you through the process"

Len put down the phone.

Del Rafferty had come across East Anglia to focus on his team of distributors with drugs he had got from a smuggling operation on the coast of Essex. Not so flash as Leppo, Del drove a second hand silver grey Toyota Prius, and prided himself on keeping below the horizon and moved around his contacts' meeting places on a regular basis. He was aware of Leppo, but had never met him, nor did he really want to.

Pure coincidence then that he arrived in West Kenning, bubbling with confidence and with plenty of small packets that were craved by some of the local kids. He certainly wasn't looking for trouble, but word soon got out and it wasn't long before the youngsters and some homeless old men were making contact.

Those who were loyal to Leppo, or perhaps just too scared of him, tried to send the toughies out to warn Del off, but Del was having none of it.

"I've got the goods, boys, do you want it or not?"

Unfortunately for Del, local police officer Toby Bunch had got wind of his arrival and found Del, just as the boys scampered off, and managed to suggest to him that it might be a good idea if he accompanied him back to the station without too much fuss. Del saw no sense in making a particularly impressive scene and reluctantly went with a "it's a fair cop, guv., but I think we may be able to do a deal. I've got some useful info you might like."

In the dining room at Snetterbrook Hall, Lady Hilda said, "You heard about all this drugs stuff in West Kenning, Douglas? My bridge partners were full of the stories last evening."

"Not just there, I know. Bloody awful stuff. Ruining too many lives, and those bastards living off the proceeds. Evil buggers."

"Wasn't like that in our day, dear."

"You what? Bloody opium dens everywhere."

"I suppose you used to puff away on the old hookah when you were out east."

"Never touched the stuff. Supposed to take your mind away from reality. Too scary."

"Not like rum then, dearest?!!"

Back in the Planning Office, new planning applications were being allocated to the staff, and Jason Quail had been given one for some new housing in the village of Swinton that Jane knew was where Jim Prentice lived. Twenty two new houses on a site at the edge of the village that would blot out the view of the church from one of the existing Closes was bound to cause a stir.

It was no surprise that this was adjacent to where Jim's house was.

Jason was on the ball and organised for the applicants to visit the office for an early discussion. Two days later he told the developer that he thought eight of the houses should be affordable for rent by a housing association. Needless to say, the developer said that they couldn't afford to do that, as the finances wouldn't stack up, and when challenged by Jason to show him the figures to support their case, the developer's agent said it would take a day or two to retrieve them.

"So you don't have these figures to hand, then," he said. "That's strange when this is the argument you knew we were going to have!"

"We'll get them to you, as soon as we get back to the office"

"Why can't you get them e-mailed to you now?" argued Jason, but this fell on stony ground.

"The other main thing for you to put your minds to is how are you going to dispel the objections from the locals. They are a tough group, and I'm sure you will find that out when you have your public meeting. I do assume you will be holding one."

"Thanks for your time Mr Quail."

No handshake, just a nod.

Chapter 12

After a few frantic days of putting his ideas in a row, Len met up with his party colleagues at the Local Labour Club. It was where the beer was cheap, but so was the furniture and the flooring, and the ceiling still showed the remnants of the days and evenings of indoor smoking.

Most put up with this as it didn't cost them anything to rent the room, but a few were biting their lips, not least Fiona who found the place "quite disgusting".

Len set out his ideas for the election in the Spring, and was receptive to many ideas not least from the members who were normally less outspoken than the majority. After half an hour, Len shut down the discussion and moved on to the next business.

He unrolled a set of plans and showed the meeting his ideas for the conversions of the Maltings, and said that he thought the principles were good and would be welcomed by the town.

Fiona wanted to know why it was being proposed in his town and not is a more disadvantaged part of the District, and anyway, where was the money coming from?

Len had to admit that not all avenues had been followed for the funding, but he was hopeful of a solution in a week or so.

She noticed that he didn't answer the first part of her question.

The room was filled with raised eyebrows.

"Have the planners been involved yet?" asked Jim, "If this thing is going to have legs it is best that you cross as many bridges as you can as soon as you can. Anyway, I would feel squeamish about you putting this up as a real proposal rather than a kite flying exercise without a full business plan, environmental assessments, traffic surveys and all the other things you would be challenged on. And.....there is a severe risk of this being seen as you having a conflict of interest."

Len went puce. "Look here, you bloody little rat, I put you in as Vice Chairman of the planning committee so that the party line would be followed, not for you to go all precious on me."

Jim looked over to Tom and expected him to take up the cudgels, but Tom's eyes were at the floor. He was thinking.

Twenty three members of the Parston Labour Party were shuffling in their seats, many too scared to openly oppose the Leader and risk de-selection for the election, and were relieved when no show of hands was required, Len assuming all would be following his strong leadership.

Wrong!

Next day Tom, having decided that something needed to be done, rang Jim and they agreed that the suspicious nature of Len's proposals needed to be fed gently to those who needed to know. He would talk with Clive and Bob, and to Terry Whitefoot to see what the reaction the top management would be.

Coincidentally, a few minutes later Jim's phone rang. It was Jerry, the Parish Clerk asking if he could attend a public meeting to discuss the planning proposal for the twenty two homes. Of course he would.

The Clerk had also been in touch with the local press, and Geoff had jumped at the chance to see how these meetings were conducted, as he rightly suspected that there would be a bit of a rumpus.

Geoff guessed that Jim would be involved and rang him.

Jim's head was spinning and decided to spill the beans about Len's ideas. Geoff was on cloud nine with two big stories about to break. And that didn't include the bonfire night accident in Dilford.

Craig Jayden was a big man, six foot four and eighteen stone, broad as a barn door, local as they come, and fit as a flea for his sixty eight years. With a huge contacts list, a great tactical mind and an attitude to "say it as it is". Craig had been the leader of the Tory Group for ten years and had suffered his first defeat when Labour took control nearly four years ago. He was raring to get back in control. He was aware that it only needed less than half a dozen seats to swing back to him for that to happen, and he had his team working on the likely seats that would be targeted.

When he got a call from Tom who tipped him the wink as to what was going on in the Labour Group, Tom asked Craig that his source should remain confidential, and that there was a chance that they might need to talk about this at some later stage.

They had known each other for years and had quiet respect for each other.

Tom grinned, and poured himself a large glass of Merlot.

Craig punched the air and thought of victory.

Avril's hubby Jake was looking after the younger boys one evening and she was having a quiet pint of lager with Jean, one of her girlfriends, when she got a text from Geoff who had been making progress on the stories going round the pubs.

"Need to talk. Looks like the fan has jammed with all the shit flying about! C U L8r."

"Sorry, Jean. Work. Looks like I better make the call."

She rang Geoff back and got the gist of what was getting him so excited.

"Do you think it can wait 'til morning. I've had a few and can't drive!"

"Well, I guess it can. I'll be drafting a few columns that we can discuss when you get in."

Geoff got to bed at one thirty, knackered but with a large grin.

Feeding off Geoff's thoughts about the gossip around the town, Avril thought that a little taster might fit for the last of the weekly editions in November:-

> ### No truth in the rumours of a Labour Party rift.
>
> *Murmurings around the town suggest that all is not well in the Parston Labour Party.*
>
> *Uneasy feelings abound and a source close to a few of the leading members of the Group indicated that there may be some changes afoot.*
>
> *However, our reporter found nothing to substantiate this, although the rumours continue to flourish.*

Del Rafferty was unloading his info to Toby in the interrogation cell. All he knew about Leppo and his operation, where his contacts were, and when and where he thought the Drugs Squad might want to get involved. Toby kept his mouth shut and let Del relieve himself of all the junk he could.

Del was ranting about the way the competition had got so hot in the last couple of years and spilled a few racist remarks at the same time.

After an hour of this, Toby called the desk sergeant and suggested that Del should be arrested and taken to County HQ for processing.

By four thirty, Del was in a cell at County HQ, wondering what the hell he had done and what would happen next. Pandora's box was nothing to what he feared.

One lunchtime, Jane was having coffee and a sandwich in the Portuguese restaurant and was waiting for Jim to appear. He seemed concerned with his brow more ruffled than normal when he came in and ordered a mocha with extra chocolate and a flapjack. All the sugar he could handle.

"Hi, Jane, how's it going?"

"To be frank, Jim, I'm not in the best frame of mind. Too much going on at work and the kids are having a bad time of it too. But that's not your problem. What's going on in your world?"

"You'll have heard of the proposal by Bagleys to put nearly a couple of dozen new houses on the field in our village right next to the close where I live. It puts me in a very difficult position."

"Yes, I've put Jason Quail on the case. I suspect he will be as tough as anyone."

"There's going to be a public meeting soon. Will you be able to come, and even Clive if he can?"

"I'm sure we can cover it, Jim. Anything else you can tell me?"

DECEMBER

Chapter 13

It was early in the month when the Swinton Parish Council called a public meeting to discuss the draft proposal for twenty two new homes. No planning application had yet been submitted and this was to be a preliminary consultation meeting.

At the top table was the Parish Chairman Elizabeth Kaye, Parish Clerk Jerry Hollis, who was taking the minutes, Paul Welham from Bagleys the developers, and Clive Painter who had been persuaded to come by Jim.

A stocky woman with a ruddy face, Elizabeth was from farming stock and helped to run a riding school within the farm's enterprises which also included a farm shop and a large Pick Your Own season for blackcurrants, Victoria plums and strawberries.

At the back of the hall were neighbours of Jim, looking in a fighting mood.

Elizabeth opened the meeting by welcoming everyone, saying how pleased that so many had wanted to be involved, and that Paul had come to explain the proposal and the basis behind it.

Jim held a neutral position in the centre of the room, whilst Geoff had managed to find a small table near the front so he could see the action and write his notes. Jason was also on the front row.

Elizabeth asked Clive to indicate the current planning policies for the area, which he did with clarity and very little jargon. Geoff was impressed. "Always know who your readers are."

Clive said that whilst they were reviewing the housing needs for the District as a whole, the final policy wouldn't be approved until the Summer.

However, the current situation was that this village was not one where the policy allowed for development of this size. Nevertheless there was always a case to be made to show that there was overriding need in any particular area, as well as a case which convinced us that the environmental impact was acceptable. Those would be the primary tests.

Paul stood and thanked the Council for arranging the event so that he could explain the project in some detail. He did so with a set of images projected on to the white wall behind the top table, and the crowd amused themselves when those on that top table shuffled about so that they could see.

He said that there had been detailed surveys showing that people wanted to live in these homes, that Swinton was a lovely village with a number of facilities, the shop, the tea shop, the church, the pub, and it was only a ten minute walk to a bus stop into West Kenning.

"What about the doctors, then," came a voice from the back of the hall, "they're all full, and it's hard to get a dentist, and the nearest primary school is full. What are you doing about that?"

Another chimed in, "and the road system is painful, on the assumption that many of these houses will have two cars, and when the kids are old enough there will be three or four, how do you know if the roads will cope – even if you care."

Elizabeth needed to get control. "Ladies and gentlemen, I know that feelings run high, and that we all care about these things, but, for the sake of reasonable discussion, please allow Paul to finish his presentation. Paul, please carry on."

"Thank you, Madam Chairman. These issues are not unexpected in any proposal, and we have spent time and money examining them. We will have detailed reports ready for the application to go to the Committee." "When's that, then?" came another voice, "Will that be rushed through so we don't have time to sort through the reports and prepare our arguments?"

Elizabeth said, "I'm sure that won't be the case, but I'll leave that one to Mr Painter in a minute. Please continue Mr Welham.

Paul ploughed on aware at mounting murmuring, finished speaking and sat down. There was no applause.

Clive stood and said that the case would be dealt with thoroughly, that the case officer was in the room and had heard both sides of the argument, and that the District Councillor was also here and would want to see fair play.

There were more questions about the details of the scheme that were as yet incomplete, about drainage and overlooking, about water supply, about the need for play areas and affordable housing. After Elizabeth closed the meeting, she said there would be an opportunity to talk with Paul over tea and biscuits.

No-one wanted to talk with Paul, and so he said his farewells and drove home.

Jim was impressed by what he had heard and thought that there would be enough to scupper the scheme, but his mind kept wandering to the lunchtime meeting with Jane.

Oh dear, he was becoming besotted.

He spoke with Clive and thanked him for coming, and hoped that the right recommendation would be made.

"I have no doubt, Jim. The recommendations are always

right; it's the decisions that aren't!"

They bade each other a good night.

Jason had shot off quickly so he could get a couple of pints down his neck before going home to watch the late football.

"What the bloody hell's going on, Hilda," asked the Vice-Admiral, "another damned developer wanting to plant his horrid bloody little boxes on another sodding meadow. It's an outrage. D'ya know what? I'll write to the paper again. Might even get in touch with the TV chaps and see if they are onto it."

He wrote a handwritten letter on his headed embossed 120 gsm weighted notepaper and walked to the post box to catch the last post of the day.

"You know what, Hilda? Bloody people round here are not picking up their dog's shit. It is quite disgraceful."

"I remember the time when you used to see white ones. Don't see them these days."

The following day Geoff opened the post and saw the letter from the Vice-Admiral. "Oh no, what's Darth up to now?"

"What are you on about, Geoff?" asked Avril. "Who the hell is Darth?"

"Oh, you know, the Admiral with the hyphen."

"What do you call him Darth for, then?"

"Oh, Just his initials – Vice-Admiral Douglas Ewart-Robinson. Good one, eh?"

As they often did before Christmas, Dave Wakefield met up with Jane for lunch at one of the pubs a few miles out of town. Dave had been Jane's boss before he retired, and Clive had been appointed. Jane had gone for the top job, but Councillors had preferred to bring a new broom into the Department.

As it happened it had worked out well. Clive had been impressive, the staff liked his approach, and bearing in mind Jane's marital problems, it had been a blessed relief that she had been overlooked.

Jane and Dave had always got on well together and whilst there had been a bit of a spark between them, it was a very dull one. Dave was too committed to Michelle to go too far with it anyway, and so they had remained friends, and Jane was not ashamed to admit that on the odd occasion she had e-mailed him for some advice on a particularly tricky situation, whether on a case or on an issue with her team.

Only a small glass each, as they were driving, but the home made steak and kidney pudding went down a treat.

"So, what's the latest gossip, then Jane," asked Dave.

"Staffing is under scrutiny yet again, another bloody restructuring, and there's a good old controversial housing case under way in Jim Prentice's patch, in fact on the field almost next door to him. I've let Jason have his head on that one, and I think the exposure will do him good.

Then there's the rumour about Len's continual dodgy dealings."

"That's an interesting mix! Len was always doing things that looked good on the surface, but there was always the suspicion that there was something in it for him. Anyway, how are you doing, yourself?"

"I have to say, Dave, that life has been a bit shit lately," and she rattled on about the girls and that "fucking ex-husband of mine". He's not paying enough maintenance for the girls and things are a bit tight especially with Christmas coming up."

"Oh, wow, that sounds like a tough time. Can I do anything to help?"

"Just be there, in case I need a shoulder, thanks so much."

A couple of friendly pecks on the cheek, and they went their separate ways.

Jason was shouting the odds in the office when Jane got back.

"They've no idea. Talk about housing needs, bloody hell, where are the needs? They're not in some little village, they've got to be where the facilities are. Does he really think that his scheme is going to solve any problems? If he's going to get away with it we better get our eight affordable houses. Bollocks that they can't afford it. It's simple really, why don't they work out the costs and a decent profit and work out the price of the land from that. Fucking greedy landowners, that's what it is.
Rant over."

Jane just stared.

The rest of the team applauded.

"That is the logical way, Jason, but it doesn't always work out like that. I know we are in the planning business, but basically we are only enablers. It is definitely the responsibility of other agencies to follow the plan making process, and to be a part of it, so they know what their investment plans should look like," said Jane.

"I know that, but when bloody stupid decisions are made by our committees that throw the agreed policies out of the window, what are we supposed to do? Are they bent or something? Are they being bought?"

"Find me the evidence of that and I'll do something about it, but in the meantime just put it down to the powers of democracy."

"It's fucking bent" muttered Jason, and went to the loo.

Chapter 14

Geoff Pulling was buzzing. He desperately wanted to author the story about Len's project, and had written a two thousand word article for Avril to check through and hopefully pass to the Editor.

Avril's response was very enthusiastic, and enjoyed the conspiracy aspects to the piece.

"I think we best push this to the lawyers, there are one or two aspects that are a bit near the knuckle. I'd love to go with it, but it will be good to clear our lines."

"Great," said Geoff, "do you want me to do it, or will it be best coming from you?"

"Better from me, I think. Not sure who's the best one at the regional office. I'll do a bit of background."

Avril got on the phone to one of her colleagues on another paper which was part of the regional group, and was recommended to talk to Krish Dhoni who was based in Peterborough.

"Morning Krish, I have a piece that I really want to publish, but I'd welcome a legal aspect to it. Local politician, Leader of the Council and maybe some dodgy conflict of interest and funding issues in one of his projects, and it looks to be a personal rather than a community one. He's has his followers, but many others are against him. Nothing new in that side of politics, I know, but there is an unsavoury air around it. Can I email it to you, please?"

"Yes, of course, Avril. When do you want my comments by?"

"No real rush, but as the rumour mill is grinding its corn at the moment, so the sooner the better, please."

Krish said that she would have his opinion within four days.

She called her colleague "Four days to tidy this and the other one up, then Geoff."

Tom Middleton had met up with Clive Painter in the Chief's office during their normal briefing before the Planning Committee's monthly meeting. They ran through the items on the agenda, and Tom then confirmed his previous concerns about Len's project.

"As far as I know, he's not been in to see any of my team, but I'll find out in a little while," said Clive, "Jane has had to take a couple of days off. She's quite under the weather. Still she never got over the trauma of her divorce, I suspect."

"Do you want to keep this to yourself for a while or should we get Terry and Bob involved?" asked Tom.

"We should make sure they are in the loop, or otherwise it will get fed to them some other way. I'll talk to them later."

"The mood in the Group is pretty grumpy at the moment, and I have a fear that things will get worse before they improve. And I'm not sure that they will!"

"That's not good for you then, Tom, with the elections due soon. I bet Craig's lot will have a field day. It would be sad to lose you, for I'm sure we've done some good work between us all in the last three years or so."

"Nice of you to say so, Clive, it has been a pleasure to see how a team like yours works."

Mutual admiration tests all passed, Tom left and went home.

In the Chief Executive's smart office, Bob was scratching his head, and looking blankly at Clive and Terry.

"So, what's the legal angle on this, Terry?" asked Bob.

"Difficult to deal with without lots of evidence. What we have at the moment is a lot of gossip, political infighting, but no detail, so it's hard to put a focus on the real issue", said Terry and went on, "is his idea realistic? Will it come to a planning application? Who can try and put a stop to it without too much public scrutiny? Is he being altruistic or is he in it for himself? If he presses on and fails, what happens next? What effect will it have on the perception and reputation of the Council? All those things need answers, but we need it out in the open first."

Bob thought a while and said "I think we let it stew for a time. I have a feeling this sort of thing has a way of sorting itself out."

Clive agreed, and they went their separate ways.

Del Rafferty had got himself tidied up and was prepared for his big day in the Magistrates Court. He had briefed his solicitor about the information he had given to the police about Leppo and his operation. Whilst no action had taken place yet, he knew that the Drug Squad had held off until the outcome of his case was known.

He had been taken to the Court in Norwich in a police van, and had asked to go to the loo before he entered the court. He was accompanied by a young officer who removed his handcuffs to allow him to enter the cubicle. He just sat and thought. After five minutes the officer called to him to come out, but Del claimed constipation was slowing the process, and after another three minutes, he flushed the cistern and came out.

There were three Magistrates on the bench; Pansy Duffield-Whyte, James Carnell and Khalid Patel. James was the Chairman.

Del's case was eventually called and the prosecuting solicitor set out the facts of the capture and arrest, the police procedure and Del's admissions that had been recorded.

In Del's defence, his solicitor told the court that the facts were not disputed, and that Del had one previous conviction for dealing for which he had spent a year in jail. He had hoped to return to a life free from drugs but had been dragged into it again by friends from coastal Essex, was desperately sorry and would attend therapy sessions. He hoped that the information he had provided to the police would allow Your Honours to pass any sentence for further imprisonment in a way that was suspended for two years to prove his good behaviour and allow for rigorous therapy sessions to take place.

The Magistrates huddled together, Pansy wanted to give Del a last chance, Khalid thought that the case should be sent to Crown Court, and James thought that the early confession and the valuable information deserved some recognition.

Del was found guilty, and given a three year jail sentence suspended for two years on the conditions agreed with his solicitor.

Del was free to leave, but he wondered what the repercussions would be, once Leppo found out.

True to his word, Krish Dhoni rang Avril at the end of the third day, and suggested a few slight amendments which should allow her to publish her article.

Chapter 15

Len had decided to keep his scheme away from the public until the New Year, and was clearly unaware of the article that was gestating at the press office.

"We need to get the party machinery properly geared up for the election," he thought.

He rang around to the Chairmen, as he still called them despite the PC world wanting them known as "Chairs". "Who the hell wants to be called a piece of furniture?"

Tom was particularly content with the deferral of Len's project and was happy to agree to stand for re-election, although he had a nasty feeling that the fuss would be bound to put the "swinging voters" onto the other side. He believed that he had done a good job for his constituents, and was popular in the village. He thought it would be interesting to see what effect this and that bloody planning application would have on Jim's prospects.

Avril was delighted with the quick response from Krish Dhoni and the fact that he had endorsed Geoff's piece for publication, but thought she ought to put it before the Editor first.

Bearing in mind the element of uncertainty, it was agreed that they should put an early "taster" in the first instance so that it could feed into a bigger story later.

The "taster" read:-

> **Rumours abound about the old Maltings buildings**
>
> *We have followed up our earlier references to the uses of these old*

buildings and can report that the local police are keeping a close eye on the properties used for drug distribution around the town.

There are also an increasing number of rumours surrounding draft ideas for the conversion of another one, but despite repeated requests for information, we have had no further clarification.

Craig Jayden was taking time talking with his members and with the branch secretary and was putting out feelers to see who was or was not interested in standing at the election. His Tory team would have to be preparing brochures and handouts soon, which would be personalised for each candidate.

His train of thought went, "I wonder if so and so, might want to have a go, or if that current member would want to stand again after her health scare."

He was also thinking about the conversation he had had with Tom, and whether Len was riding for a fall.

"What will be, will be," he thought, "no good worrying about the things I can't influence."

He went outside to his aviary and checked that his finches were still in good health. It had been a lovely Autumn, and the prospects for a bad Winter were slim.

Back in the lounge, he gave the fish in his heated aquarium some food, sat back in his recliner, and was soon snoring.

Jim was rounding up support for opposition to the housing application in Swinton, and had got one of his neighbours to front up the campaign, so that he could still carry out his role on the Planning Committee without any criticism. He had spoken to Jason on the phone a few times and was aware that Paul Welham was building up his case and having specialist reports prepared. Nothing would be clear this side of Christmas.

"Oh God, no, not bloody Christmas coming up again." Not since his childhood had Jim enjoyed Christmas. Not even when the children were young and looked forward to the day with new toys and phone calls from grandparents. But now with the kids at various stages of teenage- hood, and with all the hormonal changes that went with it, with the grunts and moans, what was there to look forward to for Christmas? Dead certain that Herself wouldn't be a bundle of laughs.

He knew he would have a stack of work to do from school during the holidays, and yet there it was, bloody Christmas coming up fast, people were looking forward to time off from work, the prospect of too much food, and definitely more to drink and all the usual fun.

"Fun? Bah humbug."

As grumpy as he felt, he was looking forward to seeing Jane at the restaurant again this week.

Far from feeling grumpy, the admin staff at the planning office were already in the mood, and there were giggles galore as Audrey and Sandra were holding onto each other in turn as they stood on chairs to put up the bunting across the room. Staggering from seat to seat the giggles got worse to the point that Audrey had to sit down, crying with laughter, and realising that she had overstepped the mark, and had wet herself.

In the case offices, planners were in no frivolous mood, but were busy preparing reports for the Committee meeting in the New Year.

Jason had no idea when he would be facing Paul again, and the uncertainty was screwing him up.

Jane had returned after her mini-breakdown and was gathering a list of the cases that needed a decision soon, and chasing the staff for progress reports.

HB was to present his report on the state of the Historic Buildings at Risk, and was preparing the final draft for Clive's approval. Photographs taken and inserted into the report would add to the clarity in making his case. He had been in touch with his contact at Historic England who was happy to support his recommendations.

Leppo had heard of Del Rafferty's court case and was furious at the outcome. He had expected Del to get a long time in prison. However, there was a bright side, in that he wouldn't be encroaching on his patch now, but he had heard that Del had spilt the beans on him.

What now? Maybe he would have to move to another county.

A couple of days later, Jim and Jane met for the latest briefing, and the last before Christmas.

"What are you doing for the festive season, then." asked Jane sipping her coffee.
"To be honest, it's going to be like almost any other day. It's not a good time for me. Zac and Philippa are

being pains in the arse, and She will have her nose in the telly most of the time. I must say I'd rather be here with you." he said with a tear in his eye.

"Oh poor you, that's not nice. I'm going back to Nottingham with the girls to be with my mum and dad. They are not in the best of health, and they haven't seen the girls for a while. It will be a call of duty really, though, and Lou will be bored rigid. I expect she and Molly will be stuck to their iPads."

"Anyway," said Jim, "you ought to know that Len has been seeking our views on his project. I said exactly what I felt and am not in his good books anymore. Must say I'm not that bothered though. I've got this case in the village that's taking a fair bit of time."

"I know. Jason is still chasing for all the supporting documents but isn't getting anywhere fast. I expect they will all arrive on Christmas Eve!"

Jim stopped for a minute and looked her straight in the eyes and said, "Jane, I have to say that I have really strong feelings about you, and would love it if we can see more of each other in the New Year."

"Oh my God, Jim. Are you suggesting what I think you are?"

"Oh yes, I am."

"Well, that could put us in an awkward position!" she said, and then realised that the words could be taken another way, and felt a tingle through her body she hadn't had for quite a while. "Maybe a bit of excitement would do me good," she thought, but made sure she didn't say it.

"I've probably said too much," said Jim and got up to leave. Jane touched his hand as he left.

The last working day before the holiday, little work was done, drinks were flowing in the offices, and Clive brought the staff together and wished them all happy times, and left the party early.

Jane was feeling frisky, still thinking about Jim's words and was knocking back some cheap white wine, forgetting that she needed to drive home. Sandra was all over Jason, and somehow they disappeared into the filing room. Others stayed, told jokes and sang bawdy songs.

Happy Christmas.

Chapter 16

Tom had a fine time with his wife and their dogs, going up to the coast on Boxing Day where it seemed that half the County had come for long walks along the sandy beaches. The air was fresh from the east and the sand whipped up and made interesting shapes amongst the dunes. Kids were flying kites, and dogs were chasing each other along the flat sand. Irene was in her element. She had been brought up on this coast and loved the big skies, the wind and the wildlife, the varied landscape from meadows and the marshes with their huge flocks of geese, the coastal woodland with the pines shedding strange shadows as the low sun went lower. Magical.

Vice-Admiral Sir Douglas Ewart-Robinson and Lady Hilda had a traditional Christmas although they were on their own. Their son Tarquin was in America with his family, and their daughter Jacinta, who had recently divorced her alcoholic and gambling husband, was in the Alps with her children. Lady Hilda had just recovered from a stay in the private hospital where she'd had an operation on her "lady-bits", what Albert the gardener called "havin' a hysterical rectory". Douglas had brought in some hired help whilst she was away and had eaten rather better than usual. Apart from an unusual wriggle of her backside from time to time, Lady Hilda was almost back to normal. "I say, Douglas, I keep thinking how wonderful that stay in hospital was. Just like a holiday, and I have to say, old thing, that Filipino nurse was fantastic. Lovely woman for someone so foreign."

They had munched their way through the turkey and trimmings and a large dollop of bread sauce which the Admiral thought was wallpaper paste, and were on the Christmas pudding that had taken ages for the flame to go out, largely because he had poured half a bottle of Dark Navy rum over it, when the Admiral yelped in pain as he bit rather too hard on a sixpence and split one of his molars. "Bugger, Hilda, I've just cracked a tooth and I won't get any treatment for a couple of days now."

"Never mind, dear there's plenty of the rum left to treat it, and I think I've got some oil of cloves in the medicine cupboard upstairs."

After the meal, he had finished the rum and was asleep for the rest of the afternoon, and missed the Queen's speech. The premature "loyal toast" had worked its magic again!

Dave and Michelle, after long video calls to their daughters and their kids, drove through the Royal Estate at Sandringham and on to the beach car park at Snettisham overlooking the Wash. The light was good and they could see the Lincolnshire coastline across the water. Curlew and redshank were poking their bills in the mud, dancing dunlin were whizzing about the foreshore, flocks of oystercatcher flew along the water's edge and landed on the beach forming a black and white and orange mass, thousands of knot swirled over the water, flashing from white to grey, and, above all this, massive skeins of pinkfooted geese flew overhead, honking their way to the fields of sugar beet tops for an overnight feed. It was sheer magic.

Avril's family had a grand time and walked through the forest to try and get some of the roast goose and all the trimmings worked off.

Jane had taken a taxi home from the office gathering, and then another one on the next day to retrieve her car, before taking her girls off to see Gran and Grandad.

Jim was miserable.

Len was working on his project.
Cass was in slightly better shape.

Geoff had volunteered to man the office.

Jason just got badly pissed.

JANUARY

Chapter 17

The new year shone brightly, but with a bitter north-east wind that was one of those lazy ones that wouldn't go round you, but straight through.

Jason had made a resolution to get fitter, probably so he could handle his hangovers better.

He had put on his old trakkies and a split pair of trainers and with a beanie pulled over his ears he started a jog around the streets and onto the Moor. There was a bit of ice from the overnight frost, and he was careful to avoid the puddles which might had been too slippery. After half a mile he had the old feelings of enjoyment of exercise and he picked up his pace as he went through the hedgerowed paths until he came out near an old concrete pillbox. He backed in towards the structure to let a couple pass by with their drooling Doberman slobbering up Jason's leg, and then decided, as this was the first session for four years he ought to head back. Picking up the pace again he slipped on something the Doberman had left behind, and felt a slight strain in his ankle. "Oh, fuck it!"

He rose from the frosty track, skidded on an unseen puddle of ice, and pulled a muscle in his calf. He limped back to his flat, swore again, and found a bag of frozen peas to put on his calf. He'd seen the footballers attach their ice packs with cling film, so he looked for some, but only found some bubble wrap that had protected a small lamp bulb that came in a big box from Amazon, and tied it tightly with Duck-tape.

An hour later his foot went numb, and he realised he had probably cut of the circulation. He got up, found a penknife and slashed through the tape with such a force that he pierced the skin and spent twenty minutes staunching the stream of blood.

Jim was feeling better now that the festivities were over, and had gone for a walk round the village. His wife, Hazel had declined the invitation to join him, and the children were still fast asleep. Others were about and he enjoyed a chat with a young couple who had recently moved into the Close and were furious about the planning proposal in their next door field as soon as they had arrived.

"Why weren't we informed before we bought it? Why wasn't it shown on the searches the solicitors did," they asked with an apparent lack of anger.

"The site isn't allocated for development. There is no indication in the policy documents that it is an appropriate site." explained Jim. This seemed to satisfy some of the irritation and they asked if it would be alright for them to keep in touch with him.

Jim was delighted to have started off the new year with a positive conversation, and he strode on through the village, across the market place with its old market cross, past the parish church and returned to his home for a warming cup of hot chocolate.

Hazel was not feeling well, and had gone to bed.

Fiona had spent the break with an old college friend in Cambridge, and she and Grace had enjoyed their walks through the colleges and along the Backs, stopping to chat with others who were taking the air and admiring the views. They had shared meals, their thoughts and a good time in bed, and she returned to Dilford refreshed and revived after the real pressure of the last couple of months, what with the bonfire, not to mention Len's project and the preparations for the elections.

She was making plans. There was a good chance that she would be re-elected as the town had been a traditional Labour supporter, and apart from the odd independent was politically pretty solid. However, she was conscious that support might slip if Len's very dubious actions did attract too much attention .

Queen of the planning administration, Audrey had taken her hubby on a Christmas cruise to see the Northern Lights, but they had failed to appear, and in her normal dippy mood she was sure she saw Santa's sleigh in the night sky. Others said it was a shooting star.

Unfortunately the ship had developed engine trouble and they had to spend a couple of extra nights in a Norwegian port before they could get home. They were fed up with the same old evening entertainment, and the never ending amount of food had piled inches on an already wide waist.

Hubby wondered if she would ever fit into her chair at work.

Len had stayed at home looking after Cass, and his festive meal had been a Christmas dinner from Wiltshire Foods and a bottle of brown ale.

Zac Prentice was bored, and was suffering because he hadn't managed to get enough weed to see him through the holidays. He knew that his Dad had noticed the tell tale smell from his rucksac, but had said nothing. "He's not interested anymore," he grumped.

He had been in touch with his mates by phone and had met up in town but needed cash for his hit. He toyed with borrowing off one of the online lenders but knew the crazy interest rates would cause more problems, and he'd been told that his credit rating would be awful for a long time in the future.

"I'm fucked," he thought, and then remembered that his mum always used to save a bit of cash under her mattress. The old fashioned way of banking!

Should he risk it?

Avril's boys, who struggled without a clear and regular structure to their lives, had spent too much time on their new versions of PlayStation that had been their presents, and Avril was anxious to get them back into their normal routines. The holiday had broken up their routine, to the extent that they had become very restless and were losing their tempers more readily than usual.

The joys of Christmas!

"Hey ho, here's to a new year," she shouted.

The boys and Jake joined in.

Chapter 18

Against all his usual motivation, Len had decided that his scheme did have some issues that he couldn't solve himself. He had to seek some help, and whilst he saw the planning aspects were less than easy, he had an idea that might see the objective achieved. He would talk with the planners, and needed to get to see Clive.

Clive had taken a long break and, despite the weather and the time of the year, was having a grand time walking the fells in the Lake District. Boy, was it cold, but Clive was a Yorkshireman and was made of sturdy stuff. The walk around Buttermere and up onto Fleetwith Pike had given him a huge appetite and his couple of pints with a liver and bacon casserole accompanied by mustard mash and spinach at the nearby pub where he was staying had set himself up nicely for an evening in front of the television.

In Clive's absence, Len went to the office anyway, and asked to to see Jane.

"I suppose you've heard of my ideas for the Maltings. People can't keep their mouths shut," said Len, and Jane shrugged as though there may have been a leak somewhere. The recent piece in the local paper had given a hint of it.

Audrey Forrester was in the adjoining office sorting out some filing, and was keen to hear what went on.

"What is it that I can help you with Mr Pollox? Can I get you a coffee?"

Len declined, but said, "I'll set out the principles of what I want. I've looked at a few of these buildings and I decided the one nearer to the Corn Hall might be more appropriate.

However, I need more detail drawn and as you are qualified to do that, I want you to prepare a more detailed scheme for it."

"Look, it's vital that you get the funding sorted out so we can be sure that it is a realistic proposal, but as far as drawing up detailed proposals for you, I'm afraid that is not possible," she responded.

"But, you know how to do these things, and it is for the community."

"I'm happy to present you with the issues you will have to address. I suggest you also have a financially based business plan prepared, and I am happy to ask Henry Bonner to tell you what the historic buildings constraints will be. If it is likely that it is not financially viable people wouldn't touch it with a barge pole, and in any event it is not my job, or anyone else's in the Department to carry out work for you, especially as I will be the one to present it to the Committee. I have to say that I am most uncomfortable with this discussion."

"I think you should know your place, young lady, and while I am Leader of this Council you should do as ask."

"Mr Pollox, I cannot, and will not do it. You need to get professional assistance and support to get this anywhere near ready for presentation. I suggest you leave."

"Mrs Seabrook, I shall not forget this. Believe me, I shall not forget."

And with that Len stormed out of the building.

Jane stood stock still and was shaking when Audrey walked in and suggested they sat down.

"Bit of a shouting match, my lovely," she said, what the hell was that all about?"

"I can't really say, Audrey, but that nasty little fucking man will get his comeuppance, I can assure you of that. Bastard."

Audrey had closed the door behind her and went and gave Jane a hug. "Not nice, especially with the boss not here. What are you going to do?"

"I really don't know, but I suppose I should let Bob know in case Pollox goes to him first. Terry as well I think. Do me a favour and see if you can get me a meeting with them asap."

Five minutes later Audrey was back and said that they could see her in twenty minutes.

That gave time for her to go to the ladies room, relieve herself and have a good cry in the cubicle, then wash down her face in cold water and re-apply her makeup.

"What's been going on then, Jane?" asked Bob as Terry entered the Chief Executive's room.

Jane told them the whole story and how she had endured the worst fifteen minutes of her professional life. She was still in shock that anyone, let alone the Leader of the Council should treat anyone like that.

"I bet he denies anything of the sort," said Terry

"So he might, but guessing there might be a bit of trouble, I had set the record button on my phone. I have the whole conversation recorded."

"Good girl," said Bob, knowing that he was going to have some interesting conversations in the next couple of days. "Don't worry. If it helps and you have got things covered in your office, I suggest you pop off home and have a glass of wine."

"Thanks, Bob, I might just do that. Thank you both for listening. It really was the most horrible thing."

With that, she left, went to tell Audrey, checked that the workload in the team was under control and went home.

This time she would wait for the girls to come home from school before she opened the bottle.

Although Len didn't want a nominated deputy, Tom Middleton was acknowledged as being the most able of his Chairmen. Bob thought that a chat with Tom would at least put him "in the know".

He rang his home number, and Irene answered on the third ring. "Hello Bob, is everything alright?"

"We have one or two tricky issues at the moment, Mrs Middleton, I would like a chat with Tom if he is around, please."

"He's getting a wee bit of exercise digging the garden. I'll go and get him for you."

"Very kind of you, thanks."

A couple of minutes later Tom came to the phone, slightly out of breath.

"Sorry, Bob, had to get the mud off my hands!"

"Afternoon, Tom, I thought you ought to know that we have had a bit of an upset in the office today, and that your Leader has gone way beyond his remit and beyond common decency."

Bob then relayed the gist of the dispute, and said "I'm not sure how we best play this. Terry is checking with his professional organisation to see if there are other similar precedents in other Authorities, but beyond that I suppose this should be reported to Full Council. Perhaps not yet, just in case he decides to abandon his plans and offers a clear apology, but I'm not holding my breath."

"I better have a word with Jim, said Tom, "and maybe Fiona, just to put them in the picture, but I can see a revolt happening within the ranks. He is making himself so unpopular. I'll come back to you."

Tom guessing that Jim was finished at school,   rang him straight away, and they agreed to meet up later over a pint.

Chapter 19

Jason was relieved to see at last that Paul Welham's planning application had arrived in the office and that the admin team were busy processing the documents, sending them to the Parish Council and the other agencies that needed to be consulted.

He rang Jim, out of courtesy really, and agreed to meet on site in a few days time to talk tactics.

Paul Welham had made a big point of the demand for new dwellings within the District, the numbers of homeless, and the fact that the numbers of houses being built were nothing near what was targeted, either locally or nationally. He had included an environmental statement showing that the site was of little ecological interest, that the soil was nowhere near the highest agricultural quality and that his scheme proposed new tree and hedge planting and the provision of play space.

A detailed survey and report by highway consultants indicated that there was no risk to public safety, and another by civil engineers showing that there was no risk of flooding, and that the sewerage and sewage disposal facilities were adequate to accept the new houses.

Jim was gathering support, getting a volunteer to organise a petition, and talking to as many folk as he could. He was confident that their argument would win the day.

His chat with Jerry Hollis, the Parish Clerk suggested that the application might be at the Parish Council meeting in early February for the local comments to be prepared to be sent to the District.

"I bet you can write that already," said Jim, to which the Clerk replied "I don't like going to meetings where I haven't already written the minutes! It's a real pain when I have to alter them."

Avril and Geoff were chewing the fat about the main priorities for reporting, and decided that they wanted to chase up on Len's ideas and the rumoured disquiet in his Group.

"You do a bit of legwork and see what you can find out. I'm going to see what the Tory line is, and how much they know."

With that Geoff went off to the Queen's Head and ordered a ham sandwich, a pickled egg and a pint of cider. He took up position in the corner of the bar and waited for the locals to come in.

There would be plenty in today as the market was in full swing, despite the cold weather. The stalls with the warm clothing were doing better than those selling plants.

Avril was on the phone to Craig Jayden trying to get an angle on his knowledge of Len's ideas. Craig had not heard much more than the tittle-tattle that was picked up in the coffee shops and supermarkets, but would see what he could find out. She might get a phone call back.

Jane had recovered her equilibrium from the row with Len, and had been glad of Molly's company and comfort. Lou had also been as good as gold, and both girls went off to do homework, but kept popping down to the lounge to make sure mum was alright, with the excuses to seek help with their particular study.

Eventually, after their work was done, they came down and sat with Jane on the sofa while they watched a film.

Next day, back at the office, she gathered the troops to explain her sudden disappearance yesterday, but there was little surprise. Audrey had seen to that.

Jim and Tom had met at the Dog and Pheasant and after wishing each other a happy New Year they supped their pints of IPA and chatted about the football results and the rugby. Then Tom unloaded the story that Bob had relayed the day before.

"Bloody hell, Tom, that poor girl. This goes from bad to worse. What's the next step?"

"Watch and wait, I think."

Mickey Grove was in the midst of clearing out the turkey sheds after a very successful sale of the stock. It was very dusty work and he was masked up to keep himself from choking. He was almost through the job when he spotted an unusual shape in the corner of the shed. "Fuck me!" he shouted, "Is that a body?"

He looked a bit closer and saw the remains of a young man, well, a boy really, dressed in a pair of torn jeans and a tatty fleece, his eye sockets showing the remains of blood where the birds must have pecked at him.

"Oh, bugger, this is not nice," he said to himself and rang 999.

He rushed indoors to tell Edna, but realised she was on an early shift at the supermarket, and wondered if any of the turkeys he had sold was contaminated.

The police arrived, two young officers in their early twenties. They taped off the scene and took photographs ready to pass on to detectives and waited for the forensic officer to arrive from across the County.

Mickey offered them coffee, but they declined, trying to put on brave faces after feeling quite nauseous at the sight of the boy.

When the forensics van arrived, Emma Lane emerged, put on her coverings and was taken to the scene by the male officer, put down her bag and looked around the scene. Emma was a sturdy fifty year old woman with brown hair in a long pony tail which had been tucked inside her white overall coat. She smiled at the officer, and asked if he had ever seen anything like this before.

He just shook his head. Emma went about her work. She saw no apparent injuries, no cut marks, no obvious blunt instrument injury. She suspected drugs, but that would have to wait for the autopsy.

She called her offices and arranged for a black van to come and take the young man away, cleared up her things, said her goodbyes, took off her protective gear and drove back to her office.

Was the lad a runaway? Who was missing their son? Was he homeless?

"And people think the world must be idyllic in rural England," she mused.

Dave Wakefield enjoyed his winter walks and today was on the coastal walk between Blakeney and Cley, a circuit he had walked many times before with his binoculars and his long lensed Nikon around his neck. Padded jacket with big pockets which held a sandwich, a pork pie and a bottle of water, windproof trousers and a thick black fleece hat.

The north-east wind was bitter, but there was nothing nicer on a day like this, in a landscape like this.

He had left Michelle who wanted a day baking and the Aga was making the kitchen such a comforting place.

Brent geese were everywhere flying in to the grassland marshes, their "Vs" gracing the sky, oystercatcher were screeching and the wonderful eerie sound of the curlew feeding in the mud all made Dave's heart sing.

A flock of snow bunting fluttered past on their way to find a different food store, gulls squawked and the sun shone. What was there not to like.

Dave passed other walkers going in the opposite direction, all well wrapped up, dogs either being led or pulling their owners along, he faced into the wind as the path turned its corner. His eyes were stinging and watering and he didn't see the hole in the path, slipped and turned his ankle.

He was past the halfway mark so hobbled on and eventually walked off the pain, found a slightly sheltered spot and sat on one of the few benches along the way, brought out his sandwich and water and took on more fuel. When he got up he realised that it had been a mistake to sit for a while as his ankle had stiffened up, but with a gentle start he got going until the path turned back towards the road, and he managed to get back to the highway without too much trouble.

He was not far from the impressive visitor centre run by the county's Wildlife Trust, and went in and admired the view across the marshes, ordered a slice of coffee and walnut cake and a mug of hot chocolate, and sat at the window checking on the birds through his binoculars.

A member of the staff whom he had recognised from the time before his retirement, when he had worked with the Trust in developing an earlier strategy document for the landscape of Parston came and sat with him as they focussed on the pair of marsh harriers whirling above the scrub.

"How are you Dave," she said and asked how she was enjoying his retirement.

"Very much, thanks Lucy, it's great to be away from the daily grind, the arguments and the management problems brought on by Human Resources idiots who don't understand the day to day pressures, so I'm pleased to have the freedom to be here."

After a ten minute chat, Dave got up to walk back to his car, but found that his ankle would not bear his weight and had to sit down again. With that Lucy went and got the first aider on site who bandaged the ankle tightly gave him some painkillers and told him to take it easy.

"Tell you what, Dave, let me drive you to your car," said Lucy and took him to her old Morris Minor estate (the ones with the wooden trim that Dame Edna called "a half-timbered car") and then to his own vehicle.

He thanked her for her kindness, drove away and screamed in pain when he had to brake sharply. "Ouch, but it had been a great day," he thought and munched away on the pork pie as he drove home to wrap a bag of frozen peas around his ankle and enjoy a good glass of Abalour malt.

In the planning office, Jane went to see Henry to talk about Len's building. HB was on the phone and she waited, looking through his books on buildings through the ages, and marvelling how the early builders ever managed to carry out their craft producing such stunning structures without the facilities and equipment we have today.

"Hi Jane, how's it hanging?" He sometimes had an unfortunate choice of words, but Jane liked his freewheeling approach to life.

"I'm OK, thanks. Did you have a good break?" "Yes, thanks, I had a nice trip to York. I just love that place with the variety in its architecture and the history of its engineering heritage. But, what can I help you with, today?"

"After my interesting visit from the "Blessed Leader" I've been thinking that you must hold a view on what's required there."

HB was enthusing. "I have no doubt that we will need to see a full structural survey, clear details of design that will retain its features and the original concept as a series of malting floors. The ceilings are always low in them, so I'm struggling to see how any modern use can be made of it without destroying the character of the interior. I was thinking of getting Historic England involved, because if a formal application does get submitted, we will have to involve them anyway."

"Good plan, HB, I suggest you do that. Keep me informed, please."

Clive had returned from his extended break and was dismayed to hear Jane's story of the contretemps with Len and agreed that he would take any further flack.

FEBRUARY

Chapter 20

In one of the poorer areas of town – and none was particularly well off – a young couple had managed to put enough of their wages and benefits together to afford to rent a flat.

It was one of three flats inside an old Victorian terrace of houses, and was surrounded by similar properties and similar people with little money.

Jordan Brooks had suffered a bad injury working for the privatised cleaning and gardening company that was used by the Council, and had received disability benefits as he was signed off as unfit to work. He spent most of his days limping around the town.

His partner, Emily Rizzo, was working at a care home for a pittance and suffered from asthma. A sweet little thing with a very caring nature she was stick-thin with a pallid complexion and rat-tailed hair. They were, however, very much in love with each other.

The flat, though was in a dreadful state with condensation causing black mould in the bathroom, broken downpipes that drenched the brickwork and seeped into the plaster of the lounge, and a plague of silverfish in the kitchen.

They had had enough and went to the Environmental Health Department of the District Council and demanded to see one of the housing inspectors. They were told that there had been a spate of complaints recently and that they would be given an inspection in the next two to three weeks.

Dismayed by the wait they asked who their councillor was. It turned out to be Len.

Len Pollox was working on his plans for the election when Jordan rang him and told him the situation.

"I will try and get round to see you one evening this week, but I'm sorry that there are so many things going on at present that I can't promise anything sooner."

"Mr Pollox, I'm sorry, but if you had to live in conditions like this, you would be getting as fucking mad as we are. You are supposed to be working for the likes of us. Please shift your arse and get round here."

Jordan knew he had overstepped, but was clear that he had to make a fuss. He rang the local paper.

Geoff answered the phone and listened to the story.

"I can guess why Len hasn't got the time to deal with the problems of his constituents, when he's more bothered by his own scheme," he thought.

He asked Jordan who his landlord was, so that he might talk to him.

"That lazy bugger has no interest other than taking his rent," said Jordan and gave Geoff the man's name.

Geoff took a few minutes to think, finished off a short article about the state of the High Street and the closure of shops, and looked for the phone number to see if he could find out more for Jordan.

He found what he was looking for, rang the number and after four attempts a dozy voice answered the phone.

"Is that Mr. Christian Grimm?" asked Geoff, and having been assured it was, he asked him if he had property in the part of town where Jordan and Emily lived. He then pinned him down to the four properties in the terrace, and then to the precise flat.

He asked if there had been any complaints about the state of the flat, and was greeted with a few tired grunts. Grimm had clearly been woken by the phone.

After explaining what Jordan had told him, Geoff suggested that if suitable arrangements weren't made by the end of the week there might be an interesting article in next week's edition of the Broad Norfolk Post.

Leppo was getting agitated and was trying to find Del Rafferty who seemed to have gone to ground. He was getting more resentful and was worrying about what exactly Del had told the police, and how long it would be before the Drug Squad came and found him. He had reduced his visits to West Kenning and made them at more random times, using different contacts and places to trade his drugs. It was putting too much pressure on him and he was getting more angry at Del each day. He felt he was about to explode.

Meanwhile, Del had moved out of Essex and was trying his luck in towns along the M4. He was on the move.

All the time; on the move.

Leppo would not get to him.

Or so he thought.

Elizabeth Kaye was with Jerry, her Parish Clerk trying to agree the date, agenda and process of dealing with the Parish Council upcoming meeting which was to discuss the current planning applications, and which would be open to the public. As well as the housing development that everyone knew about, there was one for an extension to an engineering factory which they knew would annoy the neighbours but was promised to produce two extra full time jobs which, albeit small in number, gave an indication of investment in the village and would be welcome. There was also an application to put floodlights on the football ground, and an enforcement case that had been troubling the village for ages but involved the Parish Vice-Chairman.

They eventually agreed on a date in ten days' time, and that they would deal with the housing case first as there would be bound to be a crush to seat everyone interested, and at least those folk could leave after they had dealt with that.

Elizabeth said she would talk with Jim, whilst Jerry agreed that he would notify the planners and the local paper.

In the sterile conditions of the forensic laboratory, the pathologist opened up the lad's body only to find a liver that had been struggling, a stomach with little in it other than acidic juices, and a bloodstream full of drugs, mainly cocaine and ketamine. There were no knife wounds and no suspicious bruises. His clothes had not disclosed any documents or cards to indicate who the boy was, and, strangely he did not appear to have a mobile phone.

In the scientist's opinion the lad had overdosed, tried to find his way home – if he had one – and had kipped down in Mickey's shed.

The police were informed and Toby went through the latest missing persons report but found nothing relevant. He thought that a press conference might be helpful, told the Chief Super and had a quiet word with Avril at the Broad Norfolk Post.

Toby called the local drug squad, sent them a photograph and told them the story. Within a couple of hours they sent a team to the known drugs spots and sought the identification of the boy. It was quiet at the time and they knew there would be more of the poor little buggers about in the evening.

They had missed Leppo by a couple of hours.

HB took up the cudgels with his firm hands and was going to talk directly to Len about the conversion of the Maltings building, but then thought that he would see if there were any of the local agents who had been asked to assist. No-one had.

So he left it on the back burner and got in touch with Quentin de Havilland at English Heritage with whom he had worked on the Buildings at Risk Register in the past. After looking up the record, Quentin was totally supportive of the need to retain the character of the building, for whilst it was not especially important in a national context, its importance to the town was "of significance".

Encouraged by that support, HB rang Len, only to get an engaged tone. He left a message saying who he was, that English Heritage has told him that the detailed design needed exquisite work, and that, if Len needed guidance HB could put him in touch with a number of suitable architects and engineers.

He went and told Clive, and left a note for Jane.

Chapter 21

Jim had had some devastating news.

His wife Hazel was gravely ill, and he hadn't seen this coming. It probably explained the way she had behaved in recent months. Like many of her family she was one who kept her problems to herself, and Jim had to hold himself back from criticising her for that.

He was not only feeling desperately sad for her and the family, but was harbouring so much guilt in the way he had thought of her in recent months.

It was a major cancer of the stomach and liver with little hope of recovery, and the couple of visits to the hospital when Jim had taken her to see the specialists were the most gruesome possible.

He had not even dreamed of this happening, and he had to tell the children in the best way he could.

He couldn't sleep. With all that was going on at at school and with his work on the Council, he knew something had to give.

For all his worries, Jim was a decent, caring man. He knew his subject backwards at school, and his growing knowledge of the planning system made him popular with his colleagues on the Council and with the planning staff.

He would have to give more time at home, support Zac and Philippa, and keep his job. He would have to resign from the Council. There were only about ten weeks before the elections, and he was uncertain whether to hang on until then, but with the serious nature of the cancer, he was sure it should be sooner rather than later.

Maybe there was a way he could be allowed to be temporarily absented until election time.

For reasons that are unclear, the District Council retained an estate of pre-war Council houses in Dilford.

Some people felt that when the remainder had been transferred to one or other Housing Association, there had been a cock-up in the survey work and that these houses had been missed off the list for transfer. Others thought that there had been some sort of fiddle going on, and a few others thought it was because they were of some historic interest, being one of the first of the type developed for the London overspill schemes. Dilford was far from being the only town to be part of that scheme, but had prided itself in being involved. Some of the dweelings were still in the Council's ownership whilst others had been sold to the tenants under the "Right to Buy" scheme in the Thatcher years. The historic importance of them was unknown to HB and he decided to take a trip to look at some of them in detail. He bemoaned the RtB scheme which had failed to plough the proceeds back into building replacements and he felt this had contributed to one of the reasons why the younger generation of today were struggling to find housing that they could afford. The fact that social housing was called "affordable" was a travesty.

The first generation of pvc doors and windows had been fitted to these houses, and to many more in the 1980s. These were showing signs of warping, and it had been agreed that these houses and flats should be surveyed, and in the worst cases replacement doors and windows should be fitted.

Bozzy Boston of the Surveyors Department was charged with sorting out the problem.

Bozzy was in his mid-sixties, a short stumpy man with a mass of black hair and big bushy eyebrows.

As a young trainee he had been involved in the original scheme and had since been looking after the maintenance of the Council's buildings.

Somehow he ordered too many doors and funnily enough one hundred and thirty had gone missing.

Some of the older councillors seemed to recall something similar happening in the '80s.

Coincidence??!

The continual warnings of global warming were having major influences on the way policy makers were considering the future, and Clive's policy team were taking it into account when considering the future for the area. It was something that was acknowledged as being a factor that should have been dealt with, both on a national and local level many years ago, but now it was at the forefront of planning, with rising sea levels affecting the future of low lying land, searing heat and the increased number of severe storms at any time of the year.

And then it came.

An unusual shift in the gulf stream, a series of low pressure areas that were reminiscent of the Beast from the East that created havoc in 2018 were developing, and meteorologists were warning of a real likelihood of something similar.

Sure enough the snow fell. It fell, and fell some more. Villages were cut off, food supplies were at a low level and the panics set in. It was no good ordering online because the delivery vans could not get through. The Parish Council meeting was postponed, the planners were asked to work from home, and the local emergency committees met online to make plans. They were working on the scientists' calculations that the snowfall should cease in about three days, but that it would probably take another week for folk to get back to something close to normal.

With families trapped in their homes, tensions rose and stupid things were said.

Jim's children were unusually quiet and were clearly worrying about the pain their mum was in and, more importantly what was it going to be like when she wasn't there anymore. For all the angst, it brought the family closer together. Jim's caring nature was coming to the fore and despite the overwhelming sense of worry, he was able to chat comfortably with Zac and Philippa.

Jane was feeling a bit clearer in thought and had met with her team over the internet, and held staff conferences through Zoom, which brought the crew together as well as solving the ongoing problems with cases. Publicity of planning applications was clearly delayed, but consultations were carried out electronically, and the websites were buzzing.

The staff emailed any concerns to her and she copied anything she saw fit to Clive to keep him in the loop, just in case councillors got in touch with him.

Molly and Lou were doing a bit of school work and then FaceTiming their friends, enjoying being at home with mum. Jane had tried to get them interested in bird-watching from the front windows, and what they could do in the garden once the weather turned. Before the blizzard, Molly had started taking driving lessons and was fed up that the next two had to be postponed. More grump.

Jane had heard of Jim's problems and rang him in a show of real sympathy towards someone who had become a friend. In loose moments she had wondered if it might lead to more, but that was before she had heard of the terminal cancer. Poor souls she thought, and dismissed one of her many fantasies about what they might have done. Nevertheless there was an itch that hadn't been scratched.

The scientists had been right, the snow stopped, the temperature rose enough for the thaw to be slow, but it still led to an overfilling of the ditches and the flooding of low lying land.

Perhaps fortunately, the lower part of the development site next to Jim's estate was under water and Jim had arranged for pictures to be taken and sent to Jason, who immediately emailed them to Paul Welham.

This should help knock his scheme back.

With the forecast suggesting that the problem would be cleared within the next week, the Parish Council meeting was scheduled before the end of the month.

As the thaw continued and the highways teams were moving the snow from the centre of the roads to the sides and blocking the grips that allowed water into the ditches, the flooding continued. Those living in the lower parts of the village were collecting sandbags and trying to all they could to keep the water from their houses. Gardens were under water, garden ponds overflowing and fish that were used to being at the bottom at this time of year were interested in getting out. The whole village was trying to help those in worst need, and for a time the focus was on this rather than the housing scheme.

Fiona had needed an intermission like this to develop her ideas for "green agenda" for her election leaflet and had researched a number of issues from solar energy, creating gases from water, to food recycling. Her report that she was compiling would form the basis for the new Labour leadership after the votes had been declared.

She had rung Jim, having heard his dreadful news, and offered whatever support he needed. She had made no contact with Len and was thinking of letting him stew in his own soup.

Len was doing just that.

Vice-Admiral Sir Douglas Ewart-Robinson had taken his old Range Rover Discovery out for a spin, and was enjoying the time away from the Hall and from the Lady wife. As he drove round the countryside he was amazed at the number of advertisements he saw. There were old election notices, signs for some event in Suffolk, the beginnings of advertising the County Agricultural show that was months away, a few homemade ones for village events, for lost cats and those damn great mobile adverts for replacement kitchens and the like. Once you got into town, just about every business was advertising on roadside fences, on pubs and all over industrial estates.

"Bloody disgraceful. Fancy letting the place go to the dogs like this. I'll go to the Council's offices and see what they say. No, better idea, I'll ring old Tom Middleton, he's only a few miles from home. I'll bend his ear."

The Swinton Parish Council meeting took place with little sign of the snow, and most of the flood water had drained away.

The hall was packed.

Elizabeth asked the Clerk to display the plans of the housing development, and invited Paul Welham to explain the details and why he thought the scheme should gain the support of the Parish Council. She had a job in allowing him to speak as there were constant interruptions from the floor of the hall.

Once he had trawled his way through all his points, emphasising the need for housing in the area, he sat down to a growl of voices, and many mumbles.

Jason stood up to argue that the need for these types of properties was not here but in the towns, and that the transport study was vulnerable to a different interpretation. The recent weather showed part of the site under water, that global warming was likely to produce more violent weather and that the site was not suitable, the ecological study had been refuted by the Council's ecologist and that no archaeological survey had been carried out.

With that there was loud applause and Elizabeth asked for questions from the floor.

Some relevant, some not, as usual thought Jason, but answers were given. The Parish Councillors were then asked to make a decision and the vote taken with unanimous opposition to the scheme.

Elizabeth confirmed that this was just the Parish view which would now go forward to the District Council for a decision, and if refused, the Company could take that decision to appeal.

The following day, it was chucking it down with rain when Jason called into Clive's office to tell him about the previous evening's meeting.

"Morning boss," he said, "lousy weather. I bet there'll be floods in Swinton!"

"Better than no weather at all, Jason!" joked Clive. "How did it go?"

Jason told him that the Parish Council was unanimously opposed to the proposal and hoped that the application would now be withdrawn, although he did think that was unlikely.

Clive had asked Paul Rashford for an update on the progress of the Local Plan work .and Paul had to admit that it was slow, as the research was proving more difficult than they had hoped.

Andrea was struggling to get the information regarding the needs for housing properly analysed, and the traffic survey was still in the early stages.

Paul agreed to try and make some urgent progress and to report back in a fortnight.

The dead boy found in Mickey's turkey shed was proving difficult to identify until Toby Bunch went to the usual drug spot and had shown the gruesome picture of the lad's face to the guys. After the usual shrugs and grunts it transpired that they thought he was an immigrant fleeing from the terrors in the Middle East.

Toby thanked them, he rang the information through to the station and thought "I bet he imagined this would be a better life!"

The piece in the local paper said:-

> **Homeless immigrant found dead in turkey shed linked to drugs**
>
> *It is such a tragedy that these things happen at all, but even worse when it's on your doorstep. Last Thursday, Mickey Grove was cleaning his turkey shed when he discovered the body of a dead boy who had apparently tried to find shelter. We are given to understand that he was an immigrant from the Middle East, and that he had traces of drugs in his system. What is it coming to?*
>
> *These folk are fleeing from more danger than we can ever imagine, and end up in the worst parts of our towns where they feed on the greed of others and their need to protect themselves from reality.*
>
> *What can we do?*
>
> *What can the Authorities do?*
>
> *Let's see what they say.*
>
> *We will keep asking.*

MARCH

Chapter 22

With the Parish Council clearly expressing its view, Jim was feeling ready to face up to leaving the Council. His wife Hazel's cancer was more aggressive than had been thought and she was being given little time to survive it. Jim told her to look on the bright side and remember the folk who have fought it for many months. She didn't know if she wanted that, she would rather someone just turned the switch off.

Jim had already told Tom as Chairman of his Committee, but now was ready to face up to Len. He decided to pen a letter detailing all the surrounding problems and email it to Len. Was that being a wimp, writing rather than ringing? Oh yes, but needs must.

Every six weeks or so, the whole of the Council meets to support the work of committees, to pass necessary policy decisions, and to allow for members to ask questions. This is a process that gives the hoi polloi great amusement and allows the Chief Officers an opportunity to run sweepstakes as to the length of the meeting, or the number of times so and so asks a question, or how long it would be before the Blessed Leader thumps his fist on the table.

This month's meeting is greeted with much expectation.

On the top table is the Chairman of the Council, elected annually by councillors and who, apart from chairing these meetings, performs ceremonial and general bullshit duties. This year the Chairman is Mrs Carole Eriksson who is proud of her husband's Danish ancestry but has to explain why she has two ss's. She is flanked by the Council's Chief Executive and the Solicitor with Chairmen of committees on either side.

Supporting, allegedly, the Chairmen are their Chief Officers who spend time passing notes to each other with various ribald comments or insults.

At this month's meeting, after all the formal boring stuff, Robin Chamberlain, a antipodean immigrant who has been in the country for twenty years, and is a renowned surgeon and Tory "backbencher" asks, "Madam Chairman, is there any truth at all in the story I have heard that the Leader of the Council verbally abused one of the senior members of the staff?"

The Chairman referred the matter to the Chief Executive, and Bob said, simply, "Yes."

Mr Chamberlain stood and said, "Thank you," and sat down.

Frances Farrow then asked, "Madam Chairman, may I propose that the Council sets up an enquiry into what happened, and reports back to the next meeting?"

Mr Chamberlain says, "I second the proposal," and a vote was taken which was carried by two votes, with the Labour Group showing reluctant support of their Leader. But with "Himself" unable to vote, with Jim away from the meeting, and two other members away sick, their case is lost.

Satisfied grins from many members, smirks from Chief Officers and scowls from the Leader indicate the general feeling.

Mrs Eriksson closes the meeting.

Hazel's condition was worsening by the day and she was now in a local hospice. Jim spends much of his time backwards and forwards between working as best he can at school, and being by her bedside. On occasion Zac and Philippa go to be with her for a few minutes before going to sit in the gardens and work their mobile phones.

Zac was recalling the times when he and his mum had been really close, and how she had helped him through the problems he was having as he was growing up. He also went through a phase of not knowing his true sexuality, and hadn't known, indeed there was no reason why he should have, what to do about his worries. Mum had been the comfort that he needed.

More recently they had drifted apart, he towards a teenage anarchy and the wrong sort of company and she with an increasing feeling of being unwell, but holding that to herself.

Hazel had always been a nervous and prim woman with a tight perm in her hair and seeing her in this state was a real shaker for the two of them, and they were struggling to deal with it.

The staff were kindness itself and Jim was so pleased to have this level of care for her at the hospice, rather than struggling at home.

As Chairman of the Planning Committee, Tom Middleton had received complaints about the appearance of West Kenning and the number of posters and banners that adorned the side of many of the roads. A "fantasia of fly posting" one woman had called it, and so he had referred it to Clive and asked what action might be taken.

Clive spoke with "Jimmy" Young to gain clarity on the legal situation and asked him to photograph the material and prepare a report for the Planning Committee. Whilst West Kenning had been particularly mentioned, Clive thought it would be politically sensible to deal with the whole District and asked Jimmy how long it would take to complete the report.

"Wow, to take photos across the District, to find out whose land the advertisements were on, and then to clarify the legals would probably take a month. But I'm up to my ears in the other cases. We have got the problems that the gypsy sites are causing and the time it takes trying to talk sensibly to them, to the empty shops which are being used as squats, and not least to the drug spots and the time taken talking with Toby Bunch and his police colleagues."

"I understand that, Jimmy, but there is pressure on us to sort this out."

"There's pressure to deal with these other cases, you know."

"We're going to have to produce something within the next couple of months, please."

"OK, Clive, I can do it, but something will have to give, and it's not my job to set the priorities, I'll need your decision so I can tell the other complainants."

"Give me a list of your cases, then. I think we may have to report this to the Committee. If the workload is increasing we need to tell them, and if we need an extra body I will have to talk with the management team, but with the budget reductions, I'm not confident the bean counters will see it our way.

Bob and Terry were busy trying to organise the enquiry into Len's behaviour and had managed to get the Chief Executive of a neighbouring council to conduct it. The terms of the enquiry had been agreed and dates set for the following Tuesday and the two days thereafter. Those called to the enquiry would be Jane, Len, Clive, Tom and of course, Audrey who had been in the next door office and may have heard the gist of it.

Jason had gathered all the responses from those he had consulted about the housing scheme in Jim's village and was compiling his report to the Planning Committee. This was not a difficult one, just a grind putting all the arguments together and reaching a final recommendation which would be for refusal. The grounds would be that the highway enhancements were insufficient, the recent flooding of part of the site, the inadequate environmental benefits and particularly that there was no proven need for the housing in Swinton.

He checked the draft and sent it through to Jane for her confirmation of the contents, gave a sigh of relief and started to plough his way through the other dozen or so cases he was dealing with.

Len had still not given up on his project, but knew there was growing concern. He needed some reassurance from Mickey, so they met at Mickey's house to check on any progress that had been made, over a couple of beers.

He told Len that it was vital to get the right professionals to help, but Len was still reluctant to spend more money than he needed.

"How much money have you got for this first phase?" asked Mickey

"I think I can rustle up a couple of grand, unless we try and get others involved."

"Couple of grand?! You can put a nought on the end of that, at least. Maybe two. Got anyone in mind?" asked Mickey.

"I've tried that accountant Taylor you put me onto, but he was full of professional bullshit."

"Len, whatever you think, you cannot avoid doing the job properly and that is exactly what you should do. You'll get nowhere without it. Follow some decent advice for once in your life. Not sure why I should, but I'll give a guy I know a call and see what he can do"

Len was stung by the ferocity of Mickey's words and said he would go away and think about it.

"You do just that, my friend, and you might need some specialist planning advice too. I would see if Dave Wakefield is willing to help. I know he's done work with colleagues on Listed Buildings before. There was that old derelict country house that he helped get back into shape"

"I remember him. Not strong enough. Chocolate teapot. I'll see if Christian Grimm can swing something for me. He owes me one."

"You ring him, then and on your head be it. Don't say I haven't tried to help." Mickey showed Len to his old Merc and waved him off the premises.

Grimm was playing golf and was winning his match when his mobile rang. He missed an easy putt and conceded the hole to his opponent.

"Fuck off, Len, I'm in enough bother at the moment with that couple's flat and the press trying to slag me off. Sorry, but I'm not up for this one."

There was considerable disquiet in the Parston Labour Party. A splinter group from Dilford, a strong Labour town which had grown rapidly and where the local members were academics like Fiona and union men and women who were in deep discussion. They were reluctant to leave the folds of their traditional party allegiances, but were finding the situation at the District Party intolerable and wondered what would happen if some of them left and became independent. It probably wouldn't take more than a couple to do it, and whilst they knew it would only hand power to Tories, it would probably just be temporary until the elections in the Spring.

They agreed that Fiona should have a quiet word with Bob Garner.

The Planning Committee met to deal with a dozen applications that were far from straightforward, together with Henry's report on the state of the Historic Buildings at Risk. They dealt with this first and showed concern that little progress had been made, and asked for a further report to show what positive action the Council could take to make sure the owners accepted their responsibilities.

As part of this debate, the matters of the Maltings buildings and the drug spots in the District were discussed at length, and it was clear that there was a pointed political aspect to the questioning.

HB was pleased that the Leader was not at the meeting but irritated that there was another report to be produced.

One of the planning applications was for an undertaker's new office in a shopping parade next to a bakery, which some members thought was inappropriate. One member whispered that the crematorium was not part of the proposal. Others thought it would put off customers coming to the other shops, and the Reverend O'Toole thought that the "bread of life" was an appropriate neighbour. The application was approved so long as the hearses used the rear yards and did not park in the front of the shops.

The housing proposal in Swinton, which was the cause of much anger and raised a crowd of protestors outside the committee room and a full public gallery, was detailed by Jason who, to loud applause, recommended that it be refused and Paul Welham spoke to support the Company's proposal to loud boos.

Tom, as Chairman had to interrupt proceedings to ask the public to show some decorum and allow for speakers to make their points as clearly as they could. He then asked the Parish Clerk to put the views of- local residents. Two objectors were also asked to speak.

The gallery tried hard to follow Tom's request but a couple of shrieking women failed to hold their tongues and were threatened with being ejected from the meeting. One woman was so agitated that she crossed her legs and left the room – with some difficulty.

Councillors made their pitches, conscious that the election was imminent and even those who rarely spoke at a meeting had their two penn'orth in order to try and raise their profiles in advance of that ballot.

After a full hour, Tom called for the vote to be taken, and a unanimous decision to refuse the application was made. There were cheers from the gallery, cries of "disgrace" were arrowed straight at Paul, as he made a difficult exit from the room through the crowd.

Jane was advising Tom as Clive had a regional planners meeting in Peterborough, and she was well pleased with Jason's performance, not least because his language had been impeccable.

After the meeting she congratulated him. "Well done on the way you presented that case, Jason, and for the language you used."

"Fucking brilliant," was his response and he went off to the pub for a celebratory couple of pints.

Jane went home that afternoon with a spring in her step. She had taken the bus into work in the morning and was enjoying a brisk walk home. The girls would be walking back from school today and they had riding lessons arranged for six o'clock.

Jane made them all a quick tea, the girls got changed and they all got into the Kuga for the ten minute ride to the stables.

Molly was riding big Jerry, whilst Lou was on Stella, her favourite white pony. Molly was cantering around the main arena, whilst Lou was in the other arena and still learning to control the different movements of her horse.

During their riding lessons, Jane popped off to the supermarket and got back in time to pick up the girls.

It had been one of the good days.

Chapter 23

Jim Prentice had not attended the Planning Committee meeting, he was too tied up with being with Hazel and making sure the kids were reasonably settled. The school had given him time off as compassionate leave, for which he was grateful. He had received not one word from Len following his resignation email, but had continued to keep in touch with Tom, who had told him that the Committee had expressed their sympathies and were sorry to know of his resignation.

And then, another massive problem hit him.

Zac had not attended school, and was missing.

Jim was in such a state that he couldn't get his head round the matter or how to deal with it. His head was spinning, his eyes out of focus and the rumbling in his stomach told him that things were not well. He was still at the hospice when he received a call from the school asking if Zac was alright.

Jim had tried his son's mobile but it went to voicemail.

No response.

He knew his friends would be in class, so he couldn't ring them. He tried Jane to see if Molly had said anything to her.

No response.

This was the worst nightmare he could imagine. He had lost his focus on his work at school, albeit temporarily, and he was losing his wife, and now he might have lost his son.

In desperation he got in touch with the Police and got the mobile number for Toby Bunch, rang him, told him the situation, and asked if he could help.

Toby was sympathetic and said he would send out some officers to try and find him. Zac was well known to them after a few visits to the drug spot, and they guessed he might be there.

Sure enough Zac was found a couple of hours later, completely out of it, and was taken to hospital to recover. "What on earth am I going to do?" Jim dissolved in a stream of sobs and one of the nursing staff at the hospice took him to a quiet space and made a cup of coffee for him. He was drifting towards a major breakdown, but he did have enough mental strength to remember what Hazel had said to him some years back "pull yourself together man, you're not a pair of curtains."

He rang his friend the Chairman of the Parish Council, Elizabeth Kaye and told her what was happening. Being the caring soul she was, she said that she would come and relieve him and stay with Hazel while he could go and get some fresh air, listen to the birds and revive his spirits, and go and see after Zac.

He wasn't sure if he was fit to drive, and one of the volunteers offered to take him to the hospital and to give him a call when he was ready to come back.

Jim was also worrying about Zac's sister Philippa and phoned Joan Peck, another neighbour, to pick her up from school and take her to her home, if she would be so kind.

Once at the hospital, which was only twenty minutes' drive away, Jim found the ward where Zac was having treatment and saw that the medical staff were by his bedside.

"He's in a very poorly way, I'm afraid. I think he will make it, but it will take some time," the doctor said. "I think this was a cry for help."

Jim explained to the doctor that Zac's mum was close to death, that the boy had been through some difficult times, and hoped beyond hope that he wasn't trying to end his own life.

The nurse suggested that was unlikely, and that the problems with his mum may well have caused this.

"Some kids have to find their own way to deal with such sorrow." she said. Jim thanked her and sat by the bed holding his son's hand. Then the tears came.

Then, after being told that it would be best to let Zac sleep and recover, Jim got the volunteer to pick him up and take him back to his car at the hospice and he drove himself home. Later he rang the hospice to see if he ought to be with Hazel, but being reassured that she was resting and would be alright for this evening and night, he settled down with Philippa, and thanked Joan Peck for her great help.

Geoff Pulling decided that Grimm had been given enough time to get back to him, so he finalised his draft column about the state of some of the living conditions in the town and the reckless behaviour of some landlords, re-read it again, then passed it to Avril.

"It's a good piece," she said and agreed it should go in that week's edition of the weekly local paper.

It read

"West Kenning's Shame

What an absolute disgrace that young people, trying to make some decent steps in life are subjected to the most dreadful housing conditions that uncaring landlords allow to persist in their properties. They are more than happy to collect rent and make their profits without carrying out the maintenance that should be required. You and I, if we are lucky enough to own our own houses, however big or small make all efforts that we can to ensure that living standards are acceptable, and that we protect our property from damage, from leaking roofs, and downpipes, and do what we can to avoid unnecessary condensation. The accommodation that Jordan Brooks and his partner Emily occupy does not meet these standards at all. Mould is in every room of their flat, downpipes are broken and the roof leaks. The building is owned by a local man who we will not name at this point, but will do so if repairs are not made within a fortnight, and if compensation is not paid to the couple. Our town has its problems, but everyone should be entitled to decent living conditions.

Watch and wait

Lady Hilda Ewart-Robinson was incensed, and replied to this article in a letter to the Editor:-

Dear Sir,

It is with much anger that I read your report of the disgusting behaviour of an un-named landlord. How on earth can these young folk be expected to start their lives together in conditions that are so damned foul. I suppose that if there were rats running around the place the landlord would be the sort to go round and try and shoot the little buggers and feed them to these youngsters.

Shame on you, and may you rot in hell.
Yours faithfully
H. E-R

(She had written this whilst sitting on the downstairs lavatory where the mould was growing well in the top corner of the wall which abutted the gun-room which, in turn had large areas of paintwork peeling away from the walls!).

At the next meeting of the Planning Committee, Clive raised the matter of the increasing workload on the enforcement team, which actually was no more than Jimmy and the part-time administrator.

The caseload was presented, one by one, in some detail, and many of them had been raised by some of the individual members present. Progress reports on each case were noted and it was clear to the members how much the workload had grown.

Clive suggested there were two ways to deal with this, or, he had said with a grin, three if enforcement was completely abandoned. The first was to prioritise the cases, but what criteria would they use to do that? The second was to bring in more staff. It was clearly a political matter and not a professional one.

Members who knew anything about priorities thought that the ones in their patches were the most important, others who had no specific cases thought that District-wide matters, for example the fly-posting issue should warrant more attention.

In the end it was decided to trial a priority scheme, with District-wide issues being tackled first, the problems caused by gypsies, and making sure planning conditions attached to permissions were actually being complied with.

The next meeting would identify how progress could be made, and further updates should be presented every quarter.

Chapter 24

The Police had called a press conference to try and find more information about the dead boy found in Mickey's turkey shed. Toby Bunch was there together with his Chief Superintendant and they made a plea for anyone to come forward and tell them anything they knew about the boy.

Vice-Admiral Ewart-Robinson wrote to the newspapers saying that it was a disgrace and that the poor little sod should not have been allowed into the country in the first place. He emphasised that he was not a racist, but we are being overrun with refugees of all types and colours and the country will not be what it used to be. It's a disgrace.

The papers declined to publish his letter.

By the end of the month, Paul Welham had lodged an appeal against the refusal of his planning application, and Audrey's team in the Council's planning administration were preparing copies of all the documents that needed to go to everyone who had been involved in the application.

Including the Press.

Avril picked this one up, and prepared a short article describing the proposal, the detail of the decision, the reasons for the refusal, and the grounds of appeal that Paul's Company had listed.

No commentary was added at this time, no pros or cons mentioned. That would wait for later, especially if it was agreed that the appeal should be heard at a Public Inquiry rather than by the exchange of written arguments.

Dave Wakefield was enjoying a stroll through the thousands of bluebells in Foxley Wood when he heard the "ping" of his phone and looked at the text message that had cause the break in his concentration. He was surprised to see that it was from Len Pollox, asking him, although it sounded more like an order, to come to a meeting with him tomorrow.

"Bugger that, I'm not his toady. I can guess what that will be about. I bet he wants me to get him out of some shit," thought Dave. "I'll let him sweat."

The following day he replied, saying he was busy for a few days with other clients' cases (he wasn't) and that he could find time the following week, if Len would send him details of what the meeting would be about.

As the weather warmed, Jane was starting to feel frisky again, but, whilst she had been thinking that Jim might help solve her frustration, his current problems would not let that get even close to helping. She would have to help herself for a while, unless someone else suitable came along.

Back at her desk, the general workload was doing its usual seasonal growth, whilst at the same time staff were using up the rest of their holiday allowances.

"Oh sod it, here we go again," she thought, "usual problem – more work, less staff." And at her weekly update meeting with Clive, she expanded on the expectations for the next six months.

"Clive, here is the list of the current cases and the situation with each one. It's a long list! I don't expect you to absorb all that at the moment, but it would be helpful if you would go through it in some detail. We do not have the staff to be able to meet the target dates for making decisions, and, by the way, I suspect that Jess might well be pregnant and that means we will have the bloody problems of trying to cover her maternity leave. As you know, we are reliant on other agencies to respond to our consultations, and we are finding that they are not getting back to us as quickly as they should, so that creates further delays."

"Thanks, that is certainly clear, Jane, but what are your suggestions to solve the problems? Should we work on these agencies to get better results?"

Jane explained how a meeting of her peers in other authorities had shown that it was a common problem and that targets would be missed across the County.

"So," she asked, "is it a real problem if we do miss these time-based targets? Does that failure affect the money the council gets from Government? Perhaps it doesn't matter. Perhaps we should just focus on getting the right decisions. Do we need to worry about it?"

Clive thought for a minute and said, "That's good stuff. Let me think about it and talk with my counterparts. Thanks Jane."

APRIL

Chapter 25

Zac was making good progress in the hospital despite nurses pulling April 1st jokes on him, and he was ready to go home. They called Jim to tell him, and he was feeling in a better state of mind to go and pick him up.

The Subaru was ideal for the trip and once he had explained to the folk at the hospice what he needed to do, he had time to pick up Zac, then pick up Philippa from school and take them home. They could get on with some work whilst he took another trip to the hospice. Then he remembered that they were still under age to be left alone and asked Joan Peck if she would pop in and make sure they were alright and behaving themselves.

On the trip between the hospital and Philippa's school, Jim desperately wanted to know what was going on with Zac, but thought of what the nurse had said to him at the hospice and decided it should wait for them to get home.

Philippa was ready at the school gates with her backpack filled with her exercise books when they arrived, and she went to the passenger door first, gave her brother a hug, and then climbed into the back seat.

Once at home, the children raided the fridge and went to their rooms to phone their friends. Jim made himself a strong coffee, rang the hospice to see if Hazel was still hanging on, and was relieved when he was told that she had brightened up and was in her bedside chair watching TV. The nurse reiterated the words of her colleague earlier and said that she was sure that Hazel would be able to get through the night, and if Jim wanted to get a decent night's sleep he might be better to stay where he was for this evening.

That was good news to him, and he decided to stay with Zac and Phillipa, and try and get a bit of family time.

Dave had made no effort whatsoever to get back to Len who was fuming at the lack of progress he was able to make. There was a chance that the company that owned the building might renege on the deal if he didn't act soon, and the frustration was building up.

Mickey had called him again and told him that he had to do the job properly, but Len's pig-headedness was leading to him losing focus on the other important matters, and not least the election. It was only a few weeks away and he had not yet started tramping the streets with his supporters.

Dave, who had always had a good relationship with the press rang Avril on her mobile one evening to see if she knew why Len was likely to want anything from him.

Avril was with the family in her garden, enjoying the unusually warm weather. The boys were playing football, and kicking the ball regularly over the fence into the neighbour's garden.

They had all enjoyed an early barbecue and she was on her third glass of Shiraz as she wandered around looking at the burgeoning plants with her arm around Jake's waist, when her phone rang, and she sat down on a garden bench and had a chat with Dave.

"Well," she said, "I know he's been in touch with Tubs Taylor who told him how to go about getting the right professional help, but you know what he's like, and my guess he's getting desperate."

"Thanks a lot! Bottom of the barrel, am I?"

"Sorry, didn't mean it like that, but I suspect he is wanting someone to tell him that he can get this thing done."

"Well, I might just give him a call, for a bit of fun. Wind him up a bit. What do you think?"

"You wouldn't think of recording the call, now, would you?!"

"Most certainly not," said Dave. "Good idea though!"

Next morning Dave rang Len who was in a meeting and couldn't take the call.

Dave left a message. "Mr Pollox, it's Dave Wakefield. Sorry it's been a bit late in me replying to your call a few days ago. I suspect you may be wanting to talk about your project at the Maltings. I have to tell you that I have been in contact with the owners for some time now, so I do know a bit about the building. Do let me know how you would like me to help."

He smiled as he rang off, and thought that making a reference to the owner might get Len in a bit of a tizz.

An hour later Len rang back.

"What do you mean by talking to the owners, eh? I've got first pickings on this."

"Good day to you, too. I know you have, but it doesn't put a stop to anyone else talking to the agents, and I have clients who may want to take it on if you can't complete the requirements of your contract." Dave waited for a couple of moments, thinking that Len may have rung off, and then said, "So, what <u>did</u> you want me for?"

"So, you have done some work on old buildings, those Listed Buildings with special protection, and will know the processes I need to go through, yes?"

"Probably," said Dave.

"Would you meet with me tomorrow evening, please?"

"Sorry, not tomorrow as I have an important appointment at that time." Dave was wanted in the pub team to play cribbage. "I can make next Monday."

"Are you taking the piss?" said Len, "I may ring you before then"

Dave was pleased with himself, and he would enjoy his game of crib and a couple of pints before he went home for a cuddle with Michelle. And, he thought, probably more.

Chapter 26

The enquiry into Len's behaviour and aggression towards Jane was conducted in the first week of April, and George Patterson was in the chair. George was the Chief Executive of one of the Suffolk Councils and was supported by Terry Whitefoot along with his secretary who would record the events and the evidence.

Jane was the first to be called. Whilst this was a formal event, George had decided that more would be achieved if a relaxed seating arrangement was used and they had arranged the armchairs in a circle around a coffee table in one of the committee rooms. A coffee pot was at the ready and a plate of digestive biscuits was in the centre of the table.

After the introductions and a few pleasantries George asked Jane to set out her record of the meeting, and Jane asked if the enquiry would accept her written statement of what went on. This was felt to be a sensible way forward, and George suggested a ten minute break while he and Terry read the typed statement.

"How long have you known Mr Pollox," asked George, readying himself to take his notes.

"Well, Sir, I have been here for nine years now, and he has been a District Councillor since well before I joined. In my early days, and of course his Party was in opposition at that time, I only dealt with him if one of his constituents had a problem my team were dealing with. In that case I would investigate through my colleague who was dealing with the case, and then update him, usually by email. In recent years, after the last election, Mr Pollox has clearly had much more influence in making policy, and, I suppose, carried more clout."

"Have you previously had any difficult exchanges with him?"

"Not particularly. Both I and my staff have had disagreements with him, largely over his dislike of some of the planning policies and the way we were dealing with applications, but that happens all the time, and with many councillors."

"Had you known about Mr Pollox's project before he came to see you?"

"I had heard a number of rumours from other councillors, and from discussions with the local press."

"So, you were on your guard when he came to see you?"

"No, I wasn't. I was content to talk with him about processes for any planning application, as I am with anyone."

"If your Chief, Mr Painter had been in the office, would you have been involved?"

"I understand that he tried to meet with Clive, but he was away from the office, so Mr Pollox asked to see me. Had Clive been here, he would, of course have met him, and may have called me in to the meeting. We can't know that."

"You say in your statement that Mr Pollox asked you to carry out some work for him. Please explain why you refused."

"He asked me to carry out some work that should be carried out by an independent consultant. It is not the job of one of the Council's officers to do private work for a councillor, whoever it is."

"But do you know of any of your officers who do "private work?"

"I know of one who has made planning applications, but not in this District. It is an agreed policy that no-one should do that. Some of the Council's architects have made applications here, but they do not pass judgement on them."

"Mr Whitefoot, would you care to comment on this please?"

"Certainly. Mrs Seabrook is quite right in that it would be intolerable for anyone employed by the Council to put forward a private scheme and then be a party to making a decision on that scheme."

"So, was Mrs Seabrook right to take the action she did?" asked George.

"Absolutely. If her statement of the discussion is verbatim, then I think she did well to maintain a degree of composure," replied Terry

George then asked, "Mrs Seabrook, are you certain that the statement you have submitted is accurate?"

"Indeed I am, Sir. I had the foresight to set my phone on record before he entered my office. I have it here, if you wish to hear it.

"Thank you, but I can forego that for now, but I may need to see you again. But for now, thank you."

Jane stood, said "Thank you, and if I may, I have to say Sir, that I am used to difficult conversations. They are a regular feature of my work. I have acted as a witness for the Council in Planning Inquiries under considerable pressure from first rate barristers, but never been treated like that before," and she left the room and went immediately to the ladies cloakroom where she was violently sick.

In the afternoon, Len appeared before George Patterson.

"Good afternoon, Mr Pollox, please make yourself comfortable."

"Thank you."

"Mr Pollox, you are aware of the accusations made by Mrs Seabrook against you. Would you care to comment on them?"

"Probably not my finest hour, but I do believe that as leader of the Council, I have the right to ask staff to assist in achieving sound aims."

"Would you please explain your personal and financial interest in your project?"

"I am passionate about getting decent facilities for the community, and this project would achieve that. The town deserves it, and as a lifelong resident, apart from when I was in the Navy, I want to see the best for it."

"Thank you, but you haven't answered my question." "I thought I had."

"Regarding the issue of financing the project, Mr Pollox, how do you know that it will work?"

"It's confidential information that I don't wish to share."

"Now, do you accept that the way you questioned Mrs Seabrook was inappropriate?"

"I said that it wasn't my finest hour."

"But do you accept it was inappropriate to speak to an officer of the Council that way?"

"In what way? I have seen what she had to say, but my memory of the exchange is different. I thought it was alright. I've never been the most refined."

"Do you have any evidence to support that?"

"No, but nor does she."

"What would you say if the meeting had been recorded?"

"What?!!!"

"Let's leave at that for now Mr Pollox. Thank you for your time."

Len left the meeting ruffled but still bullish, and rang Mickey and asked him to meet him later that evening.

Half an hour later that afternoon, Clive was at the enquiry.

"Good to meet you, Mr Painter, thank you for making time for this."

"You are very welcome, Sir. I hope I can help you come to the right decision."

"How would you rate Mrs Seabrook's professional standards?"

"I have the highest regard for the way she manages her team, for the advice she gives me, and how she presents her cases to the Planning Committee and the Council's cases at Public Inquiries. She has been here longer than I have, and she is well respected by staff and councillors alike. She has my complete trust."

"Does she have any weaknesses, then?"

"Well, she has had a difficult few years at home when she divorced her husband, but she had coped and looked after her two daughters well, as far as I know."

"Could those stresses affect the way she behaves at work?"

"No more, no less than any of us, I believe, but she is passionate about the principles we work to and like the rest of us under pressure to perform to targets that we are struggling to hit."

"Might they have affected the way she spoke with Mr Pollox?"

"No I don't think so, and I am not just supporting a member of my staff for the sake of it. I have to say, though that if I had been there instead of her, my reaction would have been the same"

"So you believe that Mr Pollox behaved in an inappropriate manner?"

"I do indeed, Sir."

"Thank you, Mr Painter, Is there anything else you wish to share with us?"

"No, I think that is all, thank you."

"Very well, I think that will be all for now."

Clive thanked him again, left the room and returned to his office.

George Patterson turned to Terry with one eyebrow raised."Terry, would you be kind enough to get me a copy of the national and your local Codes of Conduct for councillors, the District's Code for professional staff, and if you can also get a copy of the Code for professional Town Planners?"

Next day he would talk with Tom and Audrey.

Clive went to see if Jane was alright. He knocked on her office door, went in and closed the door behind him.

"How are you, Jane? I guess it might have been a bit brutal in there."

"Not really, Clive, I thought that he was focussed but fair. I'll be OK. Had a bit of a wobble afterwards, but I'll manage."

"Do you need time off to get through this?"

"No, thanks, I'm better having some work to concentrate on. There are better things to do than keep fretting about that bastard."

"Ok, but look after yourself. You know where I am." "Oh, and by the way, as far as I can see there is no financial penalty if we go over the time limits for dealing with applications, as long as the extra time isn't excessive, so just do your best to manage the situation, OK?"

"Yep, thanks."

The following morning at ten o'clock the enquiry resumed, and Tom Middleton was introduced to George, and after the normal greetings, George opened the meeting.

"Mr Middleton, thank you for agreeing to see me today. I'm not sure that we will need to take too much of your time, but let's see how we get on."

"You are most welcome. I will do whatever I can to help."

"As Chairman of the Planning Committee, what is your relationship with the staff?"

"Well, the Chief, Clive, and I speak at least once a week, just to keep up to speed with anything extraordinary, and we have our formal briefings before the committee meets. I keep in touch with the team leaders when the need arises and, of course, I talk with case officers about cases in my ward."

"What is your opinion of Jane Seabrook, please? Be honest with me now."

"I think she is an extraordinary talent. She sees the issues of any case very quickly and easily, she is clear in her advice, and she can disagree without a scowl. From what I've heard, I do think, however, that she is probably quite fragile emotionally, although I have not seen any evidence of it at work."

"Bearing in mind the issues we are dealing with today, and I gather you have seen her statement, do you think she behaved correctly and not over-react?"

"From what I know, I think she did and said the right things."

"So, you do not support Mr Pollox's approach or attitude?"

"As I am sure you have experienced, in politics, local or national, personalities clash, arguments abound, and people who do not like each other have to work together. We are no different here."

"Do you then believe that Mr Pollox was in the wrong?"

"In asking a member of staff to give him preferential treatment, yes I do."

"Thank you, Mr Middleton. Is there anything further you wish to add?"

"No, Sir, thank you."

Poor Audrey Forrester was in the toilet relieving herself of the anxiety of being questioned. As an administrator it was not part of her everyday working life to be under this amount of stress.

She emerged and was asked to go into the meeting where Terry nodded kindly to her, and she sat, head down with her hands clutching a tissue in her lap.

"Good morning, Mrs Forrester, it's good of you to do this for us. Please make yourself comfortable, and relax. We are here to find facts and not to place any fear into you." said George.

"That's nice, thanks," said Audrey, feeling that her legs were shaking.

"We are, as you know, talking about the meeting that took place between Mr Pollox, the Leader of the Council, and Mrs Jane Seabrook. Am I right that you overheard that meeting?"

"N..No, n.n.not all of it."

"OK, please tell me what you did hear. And where were you to hear this?"

"I was in the next office sorting out some papers, when I heard raised voices," said Audrey, gaining some confidence. "Jane's door was closed, but the dividing walls are quite thin."

"But, did you hear, clearly what was being said?"

"I just heard a man's voice shouting, and Jane saying "No", and for a moment I wondered if she was being attacked. I've never heard her raise her voice like that before. The man then left and I went in to see if she was alright, but she looked awful, so I gave her a hug and she told me what had happened. I didn't know Mr Pollox, though I'd heard of him. I think she was in shock, so I got her some water and then she told me she had recorded the meeting on her phone."

"That's very helpful, Mrs Forrester. I think we can leave it there. Thank you so much."

"Thanks."

Audrey left, went to the cloakroom, breathed a deep sigh, tidied up her makeup and returned to her office where Sandra and the team wanted to know how she got on.

George Patterson asked Terry to let him have the transcript of the interviews which he would compare with his own notes, so he could complete his report. He gathered the papers that had been copied for him, thanked Terry and his secretary for their help and left for his drive back to Suffolk.

Chapter 27

Early in the month, Public Health authorities were getting wind of major outbreak of a virus which was spreading from eastern european countries.

It was an unknown one, and the conspiracy theories abounded, including one that suggested this was the start of a bio-war originating in the laboratories of western Russia.

It was only too recently, back in 2020 when the Covid-19 virus spread havoc across the planet, and there was considerable nervousness that this would be something similar. Countries were worrying if they would have to shut down again, that the world economy would be devastated, just as there was looking like some decent recovery since that last one.

If it were to be that bad, had the lessons been learned? Just remember all the problems of getting protective clothing of the right specification, the masks and shields that were needed. What happened to them, were they recycled and are they still in use? Did the country prepare for this by stockpiling the essential equipment? Were all the testing equipment, facilities and software available to everyone?

Chief Executives of all authorities were consulted by Government, and as the virus spread over the next week through Asia and Europe, it was decided that, bearing in mind that they were only a month away, as in 2020, local elections would have to be postponed for twelve months.

Len was delighted, but stirrings in the Labour Group became stronger, particularly in Dilford where Fiona was gearing up for a fight.

"He really is making us a laughing stock. There has to be a way to make him see his foolishness, and give us some chance of retaining control. If not, I'd rather give way and fight for our people in opposition," she said at a small gathering of her colleagues in Dilford.

"There's poor Jim, who has done sterling work for the Party, and who has had to leave us while he looks after Hazel, and I know of others who are thinking of retreating from us, even if temporarily," said Jonathan Root, the local vicar and long-time socialist.

"With the one from the Greens and the two Independents, with Jim having to leave, it only needs three to abscond and the Tories will have a majority," said Fiona, "I know it's an awful wrench, but if that happens, I think we can work more cooperatively with the Tories if Craig will cooperate."

The Group was in sombre mood, but the pressure to rid themselves of Len's bullying ways was building to a point where "needs must".

The threat of the virus was also weighing heavily on everyone, and the thought of lockdown and serious illness was awful, and with the recent memories the tone of the discussion was not uplifting at all.

"I think I ought to speak with Tom and get his thoughts before we do anything rash." Said Fiona, and the group agreed.

Jane was in a furious frame of mind. John was still not paying the right maintenance money in respect of the girls, and Lou's illnesses were involving more hospital trips and medicines, and what with paying for friends who were able to "child-mind" the young teenager, so that Jane could carry on working, funds were very tight. She knew that John was earning exceptional money, and he had just flown off for a fortnight in the sun with "that bloody bimbo".

One lunchtime, she had made an appointment to see her solicitor who recommended that she contact the Child Support Agency, and she found that they were helpful but, like her, terribly overworked. Nevertheless they took all the details and Jane had provided documents. They would help as best they could, but they were aware that Jane's salary as a senior planner was as good as many in this area. Jane forced the point that John was earning much better money and ought to be paying more for the upkeep of his children.

She went back to work with a fear that nothing would happen.

She had kept an interest in "Jimmy" Young's efforts to survey and report on the issue of fly-posting and found that each of the District's towns were flooded with the damn things, and nothing had been done about it for years. There were also huge billboards popping up in the countryside advertising rural events in other counties, antique fairs at the County Showground, and general adverts, all of which had nothing to do with where they were sited. She was well aware that businesses needed to advertise their services, but there were places to do that. Anyway she wondered what evidence was there that these made any contribution to the economy?

A good chat about the balance of the arguments with Clive would be useful.

Fiona met with Tom a few days later in a pub near the Suffolk border and put the ideas to him, and to see if there would be any violent objections if she sought to make the moves required.

Tom was somewhat dismayed, of course, but admitted that something had to be done to stop the rot. He admitted that whilst he knew that Len's brother, who was also on the Council, would support him, and whilst there had been murmurs, he was not sure how many would side with him. It would be difficult to find out without spilling the beans to Len.

"I suppose another way out would be to call a meeting of the whole Group and put a motion of no confidence in Len, and seek a replacement as Leader."

"We did think of that, Tom, but thought it too risky. We might not be successful."

"I'm really not sure, Fiona, let me stew over it for a couple of days. I'll call you."

Towards the end of the month Dave Wakefield had taken Michelle off to France for a ten day break along the Loire Valley, stopping off at the little 2* bistro hotels and pubs and admiring the Chateaux and the local wines. They marvelled at the gardens and the chateau at Chenonceau, the hounds at Cheverny, the moated wonder at Azay-le-Rideau and the magnificence of the cathedral at Chartres. It was a fabulous break apart from the ferry crossing home when the Channel was very choppy and Michelle had gone a peculiar colour.

Well rested, Dave was wondering where his next client would come from, and it was only a couple of days when a landowner he had known for years gave him a ring and asked if he would be interested in acting for him and some colleagues on a proposal for a Green Energy Park.

"You bet, I would," was his immediate response.

Fiona had spoken with Mark Jameson a local farmer and member of the Party, albeit somewhat to the right of centre and who had previously expressed alarm at Len's attitude and potential for corruption. Mark had agreed that he could very easily join the Independents, and she also knew that the greenest of her friends, Liberty French might easily switch to the Greens. So with Jim no longer with them, those switches would leave the Council with no overall control, and whilst they all felt pretty upset about the whole thing, the dethroning of Len would be worth all the trouble.

The key would be to get an agreement with the Tories that there would be joint working and that some of the key positions would be made available to Labour.

Tom rang back the next day. He had thought long and hard and had confided in Irene who, as always was with him, whatever decision he made.

"Fiona dear, with a heavy heart, I've decided that I think we must go along with you. With the election postponed it will be only for a year. I don't think we should capitulate to the Tories, but aim to carry on a joint enterprise for the next twelve months. The voters will then have another chance to vote us in or not. It would be worth putting this to Craig as soon as possible, and then we should tell Bob Garner. As CEO he has the right to be involved early". "I'll make those calls if you like."

"That's great Tom, thank you so much," said a relieved Fiona.

Craig Jayden was in his study when Tom rang. "Evening, Craig. One or two interesting things going on, and a chat would be useful. What's your diary like?"

"I'm OK tomorrow afternoon or evening. Want to spill the beans now?"

"How about a pint tomorrow at, say, seven? I'll hold on to it for now."

"Alright, Barley Mow at seven, then."

Tom was already in the pub when Craig arrived, and they sat in a quiet corner seat.

"So, Tom, what's going on?"

Tom gave Craig the detail of the discussion he had had with Fiona, and the way the group in Dilford were thinking.

Craig raised his eyebrows as far as they would go.

"Bloody hell, Tom, this is extraordinary. Never known anything like it!"

At the hospice, Jim was close to a severe breakdown.

Hazel had passed away.

Poor Jim was left having to deal with all the paperwork and then go home and tell the children that their mum was no longer with them. Neither of them wanted to see and remember Hazel in that state, and the three of them just sat, hugged and cried.

MAY

Chapter 28

Early in the first week of May, Geoff Pulling rang young Jordan Brooks and asked what progress Christian Grimm had made in improving the state of their flat.

Jordan told him that he had been to see them one evening and had promised to lend them a de-humidifier but that it had taken ten days for him to bring it to the house. No work had been done to the repairs to the house. Geoff thought that he ought to warn Grimm that there would be a second column in next week's local paper which would name and shame him, if the work wasn't put right within the next seven days.

Craig Jayden had been to see Bob to tell him that there were plans afoot for a few Labour members to desert their party and leave the Council with no overall control, and that he and Tom had discussed the possibility of joint working. How did Bob think they should proceed? What was the best timing? Should there be a special Council meeting to ratify the changes? Who tells who what is going on? How will the committee chairmen be divvied up?

Bob agreed to talk with Terry once the solicitor was back from his holiday on the Italian Riviera next week, as it was vital to get the best possible advice regarding the right way forward.

In the meantime he thought that a chat with George Patterson would be worthwhile, partly to see how his report into the "Pollox affair" was going, and to see if he had any pearls of wisdom to offer on this latest twist.

Early in the month, the Government announced that the threat from the virus was now so minimal, that it might even have been a hoax and that the Country could reasonably get back to normal as soon as possible.

Questions were raised as to whether new elections could take place in, say, October, but the general consensus was that the decision had been made, that too much administration into the organisation of elections would be required and that it was better to allow the twelve month postponement to stay.

Had it been a false alarm?

Was it a conspiracy?

Were the Russians trying to mess with our systems of democracy as they had apparently with the USA ?

Nobody knew. Few cared. Let's get on with it.

However, Vice-Admiral Sir Douglas Ewart-Robinson was in a fury, "Bloody foreigners setting us all in a tizzy over a hoax. Bloody expensive one too, but I expect that's what they wanted. Bloody Ruskies, I bet."

George Patterson rang Bob back a few days later to say that he thought that the proposed agreement – if indeed there was one – between the main Parties seemed to be a most interesting way forward.

He had completed his report which would be with Bob tomorrow, and that he would not be surprised at the conclusions he had drawn.

Terry had returned from his trip and had agreed that there was no reason to oppose the arrangement, and that the next Council meeting might be a suitable occasion to let the lions out of the cage. He was also pleased with the timing of George's final report, and he prepared the

Agenda for the Full Council meeting on the following Thursday.

It would include

Item 5 "To consider the report of the enquiry into the conduct of the Leader of the Council", and

Item 6 "To consider and agree arrangements flowing from the result of the debate in respect of Item 5."

The Friday edition of the West Kenning and District local paper covered the fact that these items would be discussed, but made no reference to the detail. The back pages, as normal had detailed reports on the recent 6-0 drubbing of the local football team, and the start of the cricket season, and on page three was the following column:-

> *"The continued shame of our housing stock and the landlords who own them*
>
> *In March we published an article relating to the state of some of the town's privately rented housing. It concerned the flat rented by Jordan Brooks and Emily Rizzo, and we detailed the problems of damp and the urgent need to carry out repairs, particularly to the rainwater drainage. We did not name the landlord, but contacted him and sought reassurances that the work would be done.*
>
> *The repairs have not been made, although after some considerable time*

the couple were lent a machine to reduce the damp and humidity in the flat. We understand, however, that after three days the machine failed to work.

The performance by the landlord has been despicable. He owns other flats, and we will check on the state of these.

In the decades of the 1950's and 1960's the national scandal of rip-off landlords, highlighted by a Mr Rachman brought the situation to the front of legislators' minds.

The situation is back.

Mr Christian Grimm lives in West Kenning, and he is a disgrace."

Chapter 29

The Council chamber was crammed full when the whole Council met. The public gallery had people standing, one of whom was Avril, who thought that, whilst Geoff was seated at the table reserved for the press reporter, this would still be a meeting she should not miss.

It was traditional at the first meeting in May, normally after any elections, for the first matter for agreement was the passing of the role of Chairman of the Council to a new incumbent, and it had been agreed by the Parties that a new Chairman should be sworn in.

Knowing what was on the agenda the outgoing Chairman, Carole Eriksson was feeling hugely relieved, and not at all sorry for the new one.

It was also tradition that, where possible, the role was taken by a different Party than that of the outgoing one. Carole was a fierce representative of the Conservative Party, and so it was really the turn of Labour, and Barrie Fitt had been nominated. Another convention was that the nomination was never opposed.

Barrie Fitt was a member of the Transport and General Workers Union, an excellent lorry driver for one of the local haulage companies. He was not the brightest button in the box and, having been briefed the day before by Bob and Terry was realising that the job did not just entail going to fetes, air-shows or opening new housing schemes, where incidentally the buffet and wine was not his normal fare. He was a pie and a pint man. He was however, a very big man with mighty forearms which were heavily tattooed and a great forest of hair on his chest.

His normal work-wear at this time of year was a pair of shorts and a string vest, so in this formal atmosphere he did look a bit out of place in a wrinkled suit, a white shirt where the collar didn't fit properly, and with his trousers held high by a pair of union jack braces.

The matters for consideration today had turned this normally stoic man's bowels to water, and he had spent his lunchtime in the toilet.

The meeting was called to order by Terry, as solicitor to the Council and he asked for nominations for the position of Chairman. Craig, on behalf of the Tories proposed Mr Barrie Fitt and paid generous praise for his work on the Environmental Health Committee and his work for charity. A general murmur of agreement, a number of hands went up to second the proposal, and Barrie was elected.

Bob was beside Barrie and whispered a "congratulations and good luck" and passed him a briefing paper in large type.

Barrie thanked the members for the honour they had bestowed upon him and congratulated Carole for the way she had carried out her duties and the money she had raised for her charity work in support of the Air Ambulance.

The briefing note told Barrie when to refer items to Terry or him, or indeed to an appropriate Chairman of a committee dealing with the issue raised. The first four items were largely procedural, including the minutes of the previous meeting which were queried by the councillor for the Midford ward. She asked if the minute regarding the possible regulation clarifying when people should or shouldn't light bonfires in their gardens, and was there a minimum size of the garden involved or the amount of smoke bonfires emitted emitted.

Terry whispered to Barrie, who told the lady that the issue is whether the minute relating to the matter was correct or not, and this was not the place to discuss the implications of it.

Then the meeting turned to Item 5; the discussion on George's report.

Bob introduced the report that had been circulated to all members and to the press, and hoped that all members had studied it closely. It concluded that Len's behaviour and attitude towards a member of staff was not acceptable, that he had not been fully cooperative at the interview with George, and that asking a member of staff to carry out private work for him was contrary to both proper procedure and the various codes of practice within Local Government.

Len, who was on the top table as Leader went beetroot red. One member asked if he should still be in the meeting and if he would be allowed to speak as there would be a conflict of interest.

Terry responded that, whilst the point was well made, it was up to the councillor concerned, in this case Len, to declare that he had an interest. There followed a long debate as to whether Len should be excluded if he did not so declare himself.

Len, being Len, remained in the room, said nothing but looked as pig-headed as ever.

The level of noise was rising and poor Barrie was losing control.

As this was his first time in this role, he was also losing his composure, and banged his gavel on the table with such force that the head lost contact with the handle and flew across the room hitting the Green Party's only member on the left hand.

Barrie rose to his feet and called for quiet, and then suggested a ten minute suspension of the proceedings for feelings to settle down. He went outside for a smoke.

After the break, during which Terry had managed to put the gavel back together with the help of some super-glue, the tensions had dropped, and Len decided to stay outside the meeting while the remainder concluded the discussion about his contretemps with Jane.

The upshot of this was that Len had indeed acted in a way that did not befit a councillor, let alone the Leader of a major political Party.

Jane was exonerated, and was congratulated on standing up to the professional standards required.

Len was suspended from the Council for three months and urged to consider his position. He was, however entitled to appeal against the decision.

Bob nudged Barrie, and said, "Well done, Chairman. You should now move to Item 6."

This was the cue for the real mischief to begin, and Barrie called for comments.

The first came from Mark Jameson, the Labour member from Amble-with-Blythe ward.

"Mr Chairman, I have been a Labour member of this Council for the last twelve years, and I have never, I repeat never been so embarrassed as being connected with such abominable behaviour by one of my Brothers. In reading the report, and in considering the outcome of the debate, it confirms what I have been dreading for some time. But now, and I have shared my fears with some of my colleagues, I regret that I shall resign my membership of the Party. I will be an Independant.

"Shame," from some of the Labour members.

Much murmuring in the public gallery.

"Quiet, please," said Barrie. "I agree it is a very sad situation, but we must move on."

On cue, Liberty French stood and started to speak in her very calm, quiet and squeaky voice.

"Ms French, it is good, if unusual to see you on your feet, but please speak up," said Barrie.

"Sorry, Mr Chairman, and I'm not quite sure which position you prefer to see me in."

Laughter from the more smutty minded members.

"Mr Chairman, I am similarly distraught as my friend Mr Jameson, and I too will resign my position in the Local Party, and will sit with the member of the Green Party, who, I hope is feeling less bruised after the demolition of the gavel."

Stifled laughter.

Clive Jayden rose to his feet.

"Mr Chairman, it appears that with the previous resignation of James Prentice, and now these two defections, and not to mention the suspension of the Leader of the Labour Group....and indeed with the neutrality of yourself as Chairman of the Council, that the Labour Party has lost control of this Council. I suggest that this meeting be suspended."

Terry looked at Bob, and said, "Mr Chairman, we have a choice. You can carry on with the rest of the business on the agenda – and in truth there is little of contention there, unless members find something I have not spotted – or you can call an end to proceedings today and we will bring these remaining items to the next meeting which, if I understand the situation correctly, will have to consider the make-up of committees based on the revised affiliation of members."

With surprising confidence, Barrie said, "Ladies and Gentleman, this has been quite a bruising debut for me this afternoon, and I suggest we end the meeting here and now. A show of hands, please."

Unanimous.

In the evening Craig rang Tom with ideas for working together. He had given the matter much thought and had rung a number of his colleagues. He put forward his suggestions for the main Chairmen, so that he would be Leader of the Council, that Tom should become his deputy and remain as Chairman of the Planning Committee, that Charles Pallant, a Tory accountant, should be Chairman of Finance, that Health and Housing committees should be combined and that Fiona becomes Chairman, that Isabelle Smith from his Party becomes Chairman of Recreation and Leisure, and that other positions will be filled in due course.

The next day the Broad Norfolk Post read:-

Council Leader suspended

In a sad day for local government, Parston District Council yesterday received a report of an enquiry into the behaviour of Mr Leonard Pollox, the Labour Leader of the Council.

The report declared that the bullying manner he used in trying to persuade a planning officer of the Council to carry out work for him on a personal project was inappropriate and was clearly against the Codes of Conduct in place within the Council. He was suspended from all Council activities for three months. Chief Executive Officer, Bob Garner, said that this was indeed a sad day for the Council, and he hoped that it would serve to show that no matter who the councillors were, there was no place for such a set of completely outrageous acts.

Mr Pollox does have the right of appeal, and we will keep you informed of any further action.

Chapter 30

Hazel's funeral was a very sombre affair. None of this "celebration of a life well lived" stuff, just very normal, very sombre. Many from the village were in the church and the Vicar read the usual prayers and recitations. Jim was popular in the village and the church was full of residents, parish councillors, and representatives of the District Council, paying their respects to a recent councillor. Jane was at the back, standing with Clive. She wept and wrung her hands so hard that the damp tissue she was holding was ripped away and fell to the floor in small pieces. It was unfortunate that it looked like confetti.

Zac was red-eyed and was clearly suffering badly, while Philippa clung on to Jim, tears flowing freely. Jim was not up to giving any sort of speech, but his friend and past colleague Tom Middleton gave a eulogy that was full of praise for the couple, but no jokes. Hazel was not a jokes person.

The wake was in the large room at the local pub, where the usual fare of vol-au-vents, small sausages, cheese cubes on cocktail sticks, and some bought-in samosas. The beer was flowing and the warm white wine was sipped. There were no further speeches.

Before she left, Jane went to Jim and gave him a hug, and whispered, "let's have a coffee somewhere soon."

"Oh, thanks, that would be lovely," stammered Jim and turned to be with his children.

Emily Rizzo was sick. She was sneezing and was breathless, and Jordan thought it was probably hay-fever as the pollen levels had been very high. Her painfully thin body and poor diet had left her weak and susceptible to infection.

The ten year old de-humidifier that Christian Grimm had lent them still wasn't working properly. It wasn't very efficient and cost a fortune to run, so Jordan had made sure it was rarely in use. Despite the slightly warmer weather the flat was still mouldy.

One morning Jordan realised that Emily was worse and rang the emergency services, and within three minutes a paramedic team arrived, took her temperature, listened to her bony chest, took her blood pressure and called the ambulance to take her to the hospital.

It was one of the few times that there wasn't a queue to discharge the patient from the ambulance into A&E, where the doctors carried out similar tests and confirmed that she had a serious and dangerous form of pneumonia. She was sent to the respiratory ward where she was placed on a drip and given a course of antibiotics. It took four days for her to recover sufficiently to be able to return home, but Jordan had told the hospital staff about the state of the flat, and the nurses arranged for social services to be asked if alternative accommodation could be found.

Whilst that investigation was taking place Jordan rang Geoff and told him the story.

Temporary accommodation was found for them in a bed and breakfast house, and they moved their few belongings, settled down for a cuddle and some fish and chips.

Dave was in his conservatory watching the fluffy baby starlings squabbling, squawking and being fed by their parents and was excited about the green energy projects. Michelle was sitting with him moaning about the pigeons in the garden "Bloody pigeons. Look, Dave, look at them randy buggers chasing each other, bloody tails up, flapping at each other, and then shitting in my bird bath."

"Yes, dear," said Dave and went back to reading the paper.

He had met with Jens Van der Vaart the Dutch specialist in waste food collection and its conversion to electricity, and with another Chinese company who specialised in solar energy schemes and the use of that electricity to convert water to hydrogen and oxygen.

Engineers were involved in understanding the amount of traffic likely to be needed to transport the amount of waste, alterations to the road layout, expert engineers in electrical supplies were examining the amount of electricity likely to be generated and the best place to connect to the Grid, environmental specialists were looking at the way the development would be able to fit into the landscape, pollution experts looked into any likely problems in the operation of the scheme, lawyers, ecologists, archaeologists, the whole shooting match to provide expert input to the proposal.

It would take at least a month to prepare all the plans and documents to submit to both Councils as it was clear that the County Council as Waste Disposal Authority as well as the District would need to be involved. Dave's research had astounded him. Nearly a third of all food produced globally was thrown away, and over £7 million is discarded in the UK alone. This was madness and Dave was loving the excitement of a scheme that might just help not only in this locality but perhaps the whole of East Anglia. The amount of food going to landfill was extraordinary and only aided the creation of methane. His spark for a really creative project had lifted his mood and enthusiasm.

Jane and Clive had reconvened with "Jimmy" Young and were astonished by the number of photographs he had taken of advertisements that should have been the subject of applications for Consent to Display.

"I guessed it was bad, but not to this extent," said Clive. "Any ideas how best to deal with this, Jane?"

"Good God, no, not to this extent. We could write to all the owners of the sites, but it will be a hell of a job to find out who they are. We could contact the advertisers themselves and invite applications, but what policy do we use to judge them by? We could just take them all down and ask the advertisers to pick them up, but there's a real risk of confrontation."

"I'll work with Jimmy and prepare a report for the Committee."

Under the cloud that he had brought upon himself, Len was thinking how to proceed with his Maltings project. He was having a few moments of weakness and even thought for one moment that other people might have been right. It was not in his nature to admit it, so he dismissed the idea as ridiculous. He was right. He had to be.

Mickey Grove had been wary of keeping his

Involvement and had told Len that he didn't think he could help any more unless Len changed tack and started taking the advice that so many people had offered. He was steering clear.

With the reduction in time that he now had to deal with Council business, Len decided to throw himself into a last gasp attempt to get his Maltings project out in the open and submitted as a set of planning applications. He <u>would</u> seek help.

In the meantime, though, he would take Cass to get some sun.

The house had been left to Jane in the divorce settlement, and John had made sure she understood the financial benefits of that. She could always take out a mortgage rather than keep pestering him for more money. That didn't stop her thinking of the future for her girls, and she knew she had to press on with the CSA.

She had taken the day off and it was a hot one. The warmth was having a certain effect on her, and she had relieved her sexual frustration with a Polish craftsman who was laying brick-weave paving on the short drive of her house. He worked for an Irishman who dropped him off in the morning with all the required materials. The Pole - and Jane thought afterwards that it was an appropriate name for him - made good use of his break-time from laying the drive, and laid into Jane with some ferocity.

Her smile was back.

Chapter 31

Elizabeth Kaye's life was good. She and her husband ran the small farm and they made a decent profit each year, thanks to the accountant juggling the various aspects of the farm. It certainly helped that the riding school was not making much of a profit! It was managed by Charley Buckle who was a trained instructor and who was helped in the office by old Bobby Ratcliffe, a lifelong man of the countryside. Bobby was born seventy years ago in the same village where Mickey Groves lives now. Their families had always been close, and Mickey and Bobby often shared an hour or two over a couple of pints.

Charley was twenty four, and had loved working with the ponies since she had started riding at the school when she was a youngster. A long haired blonde with bright blue eyes, she was a friendly but strict teacher and got good results.

The ponies were in good shape for the time of the year apart from Stella who was suffering from colic. Charley spoke with Elizabeth and they agreed that they would call the vet tomorrow.

However, in the early hours of the morning Elizabeth was woken to the sounds of fire raging, and sure enough, there were flames coming from the hay store and sparks were flying in the wind towards the stables. Those ponies that were not out in the paddocks were panicking within their stables, kicking at the walls and whinnying in a screaming chorus. Bobby was in one of the nearby estate cottages and strode out to the yard to try and release the ponies into the paddocks. He managed to free them all apart from Stella.

Elizabeth was distraught, but saved ringing Charley, who lived five miles away, until the morning. She tried to nurse Stella but the flames were getting close and they struggled to get her up and to move her to a shed near the house. The hay store was destroyed, but most of the stables were undamaged, and the morning brought a more realistic view of the problems. Elizabeth had called Charley at six-thirty and warned her of the problem, that their priority would be the assessment of the animals, and suggested that all lessons should be postponed for the day until they had clarity on the situation.

They called the vet, partly to look at Stella but also to run the rule over the rest of the ponies, and Charley spent the first hour ringing clients and telling them the news.

One of them was Lou Seabrook. Stella was her favourite.

Jasper the vet arrived at ten thirty, and found that, apart from Ronty, all the ponies were fit to be ridden. Stella, however, had worsened over night. The shock had damaged her further, and Jasper recommended that she be put to sleep.

Charley texted Jane, asking her to tell Lou.

Harrison Richards was a wealthy man. He had made his fortune from steel production and the connection to the wind farm industry on the east coast.

His estate at Rushmoor Hall in the east of the County was well known for holding a major music festival in the summer. He also ran a steam rally weekend where many Victorian machines smoked, blew and puffed their way round the arenas, or were stationary and just showing off the well polished detail of their workings.

The music festival was held a few weeks earlier than usual this year and it drew thousands to the various stages where the visitors were bouncing around and waving their flags and banners.

Zac Prentice and his mates were there enjoying old style rock and roll, smoking weed and knocking back cider. Tam McAdam, a twenty year old scot with ginger hair and a fine beard kept himself topped up with scotch and Irn-bru. After dusk, Tam went back to their base, tripped over the guy rope of a neighbouring tent and fell onto an upturned tent peg which threw him sideways onto a metal peg from another tent which went through his throat. The rest of his friends were dancing and drinking and returned to their base three hours later to find their friend unconscious and lying in a pool of blood. No-one else had seen him, and Zac ran to the Ambulance which was stationed a few hundred yards away, called for help and within minutes Tam was declared dead.

The police were soon at the scene, and the gang of mates were called together to tell the police what they knew of the accident – assuming that is what it was – but most of them were incapable of giving lucid answers. Assuming they were either drunk or drugged or both, the police took them to the mobile police station and sat them down, gave them water and asked if they wanted to stay and sober up or go to the local station. As they were many miles from home they took the first option and hoped to have clearer heads in an hour or so.

At dawn, the music was still thumping away, the lads were suffering with massive hangovers, but were able to focus on what happened.

As it was, none of the group were at the scene, so could only explain the situation up to when Tam left them. They had assumed that he had gone to the toilets, got lucky with some girl and gone off with her.

The police had asked that the group of mates report to the County Police HQ to make statements and so Zac had to tell Jim what had happened, once he got home. He said he was sorry. Yet again he had been at the wrong place at the wrong time and that he needed to go to make a statement.

Philippa had gone to stay the evening at a friend's home, and Jim took Zac to the County HQ, where they drove through the automatic double steel gates with a communications patch, and walked to the main doors where again there was a security pad, and into the waiting space. They had announced their arrival and the reason for the attendance, and it was another forty minutes before an officer came. Jim was allowed to be with Zac as an "appropriate adult" and after Zac's fingerprints were taken they were ushered into an interview room where Zac was questioned about the day and evening. He was asked to agree a statement taken from his answers. He signed it, and looking sheepishly he turned to his dad, and asked to be taken home.

JUNE

Chapter 32

Jane was working on a scheme to allow simple planning applications to be dealt with by some of the experienced administrative staff who knew how the system worked. They also knew the governing policies which would affect those proposals, and she had allocated the new case work.

One new and very interesting proposal was a preliminary idea for a green energy centre which would see solar energy used to convert water into hydrogen and oxygen, as well as a major food waste processing operation which would create electricity for the National Grid. She was tempted to deal with it herself, but thought it would be a good case for Tony Chaplin to deal with.

Tony was a West Midlands man in his late thirties and had worked in both urban and rural authorities as well as a two year sabbatical with the Environment Agency. His contacts were strong and his knowledge of sustainable and environmental issues was not bettered in the department.

He was as pleased as punch to have such an interesting scheme to get his teeth into.

Raj Hossein had been with the team for two years and was given an application to demolish the only pub in the village of Hayle and build seven houses on the site to deal with. Raj would start off the processing and research into other similar cases to see how best to identify the issues, and would then check back with Jane.

The Golden Horseshoe had been a thriving centre of the village, offering great food, good beers and wine as well as being a welcoming centre for the community.

When the owners had left for a bigger premises with the potential for a greater turnover, it was bought by a Scot, Davie McDonald. Somehow he had gained the nickname of "Thrush", although no one in the village knew how he came by it. It certainly wasn't anything to do with his singing.

"Thrush" turned it into a drinking parlour which none of the locals wanted, apart from a couple of the local farmhands. There was no chef, so no decent food and consequently trade went downhill fast. Hence the application as he claimed the place wasn't viable.

Avril was furious. As it was her village, she knew most folk there, and she knew that they had been massively disappointed when the previous owners left. She was convinced that the evidence of that time showed that the pub could be viable if it was run properly.

Geoff Pulling was putting his mind to the story of poor Emily Rizzo.

He wondered if the Local Authority was aware of the state of the flat, but he knew that as the same Council had placed the couple in a Bed & Breakfast accommodation, they must be. He rang and only managed to get through to someone who was just taking messages and said that she was sorry but all the field officers were out dealing with others who were in similar trouble. She would ask someone to call him back.

Geoff knew that Fiona was now chairman of the committee dealing with these sort of matters and thought that if he hadn't heard by the morning he would get in touch with her. No-one had rung him, so he rang Fiona and told her the story, how Len had been no help to the couple and said he would be writing a further column in the next edition of the paper.

It read;

> **"Lousy housing conditions lead to hospital**
> *The sorry story of the irresponsible landlord Christian Grimm gets more intense. Young Emily Rizzo suffered an awful attack of pneumonia and spent four nights in hospital. The care she received was first rate, and she and her partner, Jordan, have been accommodated in a Bed and Breakfast hotel at a cost to the Council. Her treatment in hospital was at a cost to the NHS.*
>
> *All are avoidable costs to the public purse. To your rates and taxes. All because Mr Grimm did not show a proper duty of care to his tenants. We now understand that he may be prosecuted under Health and Safety and Housing Acts.*
>
> *Again watch and wait*

Jim Prentice was recovering from the sadness of losing his wife, and was spending time walking around the village trying to get up mental strength to go back to work at the High School. He had rung Jane to see if she was up to having a coffee one evening. She was happy to try and help Jim and had not expected it to lead to anything.

She would have to arrange for someone to sit with the girls, unless perhaps, they would think of having a sleep-over with their friends.

Jane was still battling away with the Child Support Agency trying to get them to examine John's bank accounts to establish what he ought to be paying as maintenance for the girls. The Agency was more busy than ever and Jane's frustration was building up. She may have to call her MP to try and get things moving, although she suspected there were worse cases than hers, with some poor poverty ridden wretch having to look after her four kids with barely two pennies to rub together. However, nothing ventured nothing gained, she rang the CSA office and did manage to get through to her case officer and was able to get her to try and push forward her case with some urgency. Two days later Jane got a call to say that further investigation of John's circumstances had been authorised and that detailed work would start in a fortnight. She was quick to say, "Thanks, and will you contact me once the work has started, please?"

Jason was working on his statement for the Public Inquiry into the Council's refusal to grant the housing scheme in Swinton. He reckoned that whilst he would put the bones of the planning case in a simple series of bullet points, he would be able to brief Jim and the Parish Council how to put their comments to the independant Planning Inspectorate, which would consider the case, and make the decision.

There was always more than one way to skin this particular cat.

So, as well as preparing the formal statement, he was drawing up briefing papers to give to the people of the Parish. This would enable the local feelings to be expressed but within the confines of planning legislation, so that the points made would be justifiable and relevant. In particular, they should emphasise the difficulties in getting appointments at doctors, dentists, and the facilities and availability of spaces in the primary and secondary schools. These would be more passionately presented by locals. He suggested that they all write separate letters to the Inspectorate.

The appeal would be heard in late July.

Geoff Pulling was reporting on the case and was looking forward to experiencing a formal Inquiry. He was writing up the early parts of the story and thought he would try and talk with Jason.

"Morning Jason," he said once he had got through to him after four attempts, "I wonder if we could talk over those parts of the case at Swinton that I can't get my head round. Do you have a few minutes?"

"I do, but what is it you need that hasn't been in the reports and heard during the debates?"

"The ownership of the land. The application says it is the hands of a Trust. Do you know any more?"

"No, I don't, why do you ask? What relevance is that to the case?"

"It's just that it's odd that the applicants are a company that isn't local."

"Anyone can make an application on any land as long as they notify the owners," said Jason, "and unless that information isn't true then it's a legal application."

"But I think we should know more. It is in the public interest."

"Geoff, please, who on earth do you think I work for?"

"Oh, well, yes, I see. Thanks"

Tony Chaplin was getting his teeth into the application for the Green Energy project and was pleased to know that Dave Wakefield was acting as planning agent for the two clients who were joint applicants. The figures were staggering, but so was the size of the equipment. Anaerobic digesters, silos for the waste food, crops of maize, waste liquids and, unbelievably, litres and litres of alcohol which were being rebranded. It was cheaper to throw it away than to take off the labels and put new ones on.

The silos feed the digester which produces a biogas that has to be cleaned in another large tank and then is pumped to a combined heat and power unit where electricity is produced and added to the National Grid. The residue from the digester is transferred to a solids separation tank so that the liquid is stored ready for transportation in agricultural tankers to be sprayed on the fields. The remaining solids are readied for collection by trailers for spreading on the fields as a fertiliser.

So, lots of metal tanks and silos, a significant impact on the landscape and a huge amount of traffic. Finding the right site would be crucial and Tony was wondering if, indeed, this was the right site. There would be a lot more work required if this was to work out.

He'd better get a meeting organised with Dave, and see if he has got other clients with land in the ideal location.

Chapter 33

It was such a lovely fresh summer morning that the Lady Hilda had asked the Vice-Admiral if they might go out for a drive, perhaps to the coast. He finished his plate of kedgeree, allowed her to take the dishes away and stack them in the newly acquired dishwasher in the scullery and went upstairs to the "heads" as he still called them, read the paper and relieved himself with a measure of pleasure. He put on a casual shirt and went down to the garage and got the Bentley round to the front door.

They were thirty minutes away from home and on their way to the coast near Sandringham when there was a fearful bump and Hilda squealed "What the hell was that, Douglas?"

"How do I bloody know? I'll get out and have a look."

Twenty yards back was a huge pothole in the centre of the road and he had punctured the front offside tyre.

"Oh, Jesus bloody wept," he shouted. "Better get the RAC out to sort this bugger." He had no mobile phone, and so he got Hilda to try and get through. No signal.

"Oh, Christ on a bike. What now?"

"Well, we can drive on gently and ruin the tyre or we can walk to find the nearest house."

"Have we got a decent map in the car?"

Just as they were making a decision a car approached in the opposite direction, stopped and saw the problem. The driver made himself known and asked if they had a spare tyre and a jack, looked in the boot and found what he was looking for. He jacked up the car to allow the wheel to be just touching the ground, and tried to loosen the wheel nuts. They were jammed tight and however much effort he put in, the nuts would not budge. Douglas told him that Hilda's phone had no signal, so he tried his own phone and managed a single bar. "We'll give it a try," he said and Hilda gave him the number to call. Needless to say it cut out part way through the conversation, but sufficient information had been given, and the RAC would be on their way. Douglas tried to give the man a fiver for his troubles, but he wouldn't take it, and he got back in his car and drove off wishing them good luck.

They waited forty minutes in the sun. Hot and very irritated, the Vice-Admiral moaned, "Bloody state of the roads, highways officers should be shot. How much longer have we got to wait here? And look along the road there, frigging traffic lights round some roadworks, and nobody there. Not doing anything. Bloody highways!!"

The RAC man was politeness itself while Douglas chuntered away. Hilda looked the other way. In ten minutes the job was done thanks to a special tool to get the nuts off the wheel. The RAC man looked at the spare wheel and did one of those "tut tuts" and shook his head, and told them to go back home very gently and get their normal garage to sort the problem later.

They both said their thanks as he drove off, only for Douglas to let fly with another "Bugger and bollocks."

This June was incredibly hot, and it was having a bad effect on many people's state of mind. Many were getting hot, others getting hot and bothered, and the stink from the poultry factory on the Suffolk border was becoming more intense by the day. The Environmental Health people went out to see what might be done, and didn't help the matter when one of them, young Polly Dingle, said that "you can't catch anything through smells".

The factory was sited away from any housing estates, but a few former farm workers' cottages were now owned by people looking for a bit of peace and quiet, some of them as second homes. One of these was Rose Cooper who complained vociferously that she hadn't spent a fortune to live here and have to put up with that sort of smell inserted into her environment. It was a disgrace, and what are you going to do about it? Polly asked, "When you bought your house did you understand that in this part of the world, much of the economy revolved around producing food for you to eat, and that sometimes agricultural smells and noises might get up some peoples noses? Oh, and I do hope that that cockerel crowing doesn't upset you too much."

Rose pulled herself up to her full five foot one and looked up at the officer in the eye and said, "You do know who I am, young lady, I trust."

"Actually, I don't, but the point is the same whoever you are."

"Look, I am the former wife of an MP, and I know a bit about this sort of thing," said Rose, "and I have contacts in high places. I shall get this reported and then you will find out what you had better do to sort this out." With that she got into her new Land Rover and drove away.

Polly thought, "Can't imagine how she is the former wife of anyone!"

When she got back to her desk she slipped into the planning office and saw that most of the team were out on site, but Jason was at his desk bashing away at the documents for the appeal.

"Hi Jay, how's it going? I've just been to see some snotty people who are moaning about the smell from the poultry plant down in Forest Plain. Do you know anything about it from the planning perspective?"

"Not much, Pol, it's not been in my patch, but there are loads of these across the County, as you know. Depends what is causing the smell. Is it the abattoir or the processing and cooking plant? I suspect the problems are about their control of the processing, which is outside my remit. Down to you, my friend, I think!"

"Thanks a bunch, pal. This is one for my boss, I think. See you."

The next day Jason raised the matter with Jane, who said that is was not a matter for the team to worry about at this stage and to leave it to the Health team.

Two weeks later some unrelated but isolated poultry farm sheds were targeted by protestors who were concerned about the conditions in which the birds were grown. There were four sheds each with some twenty five thousand birds that were grown on from the day- old poults they arrived as. They were fed and watered for six weeks before being ready for transfer and slaughter.

This was standard practice within the industry and was monitored by independent agencies. All proper and above board, but totally opposed by the protesters.

At the farm, the CCTV system had, hopefully, recorded the protesters who had tried to get into the sheds to release the birds, but had failed in their attempts. They had to make do with daubing slogans on the buildings. The police had been called but the protesters were far away by then. However, they had been in touch with the press and had sent photographs of their work.

Avril thought this would make a bit of a story and wrote:

Smells lead to slogans?

This week the heat got to people. It also got to the poultry.

The poultry processing plant in Forest Plain was going full pelt and the heat had affected the ventilation system meaning that for miles around the stench was nauseating. Mrs Rose Cooper was incensed and had called out the Council's Environmental Health Inspector. "See if you like it, see if anyone would like it. It's disgusting," she said.

A few days later, whether prompted by these concerns or not, a poultry farm a few miles away was targeted by protesters, and the sheds daubed with slogans against the cruelty to the birds. We understand that both the Council and the Police are investigating.

"I see Rose has been stirring things up again," said Lady Hilda Ewart-Robinson as she read the news out to the Vice-Admiral.

"What's she up to this time, old thing? She got too used to being in the spotlight when she was married to that useless MP husband of hers. Total toss-pot that man, just used to turn up to parliament so he could claim his allowances. Barely said a thing. Bloody useless man."

"I know, dear, but she may have a point. The way those birds are treated is awful."

"Bloody stuff is tasteless. The only decent thing you can do with them is to make a good old madras curry. Can't taste the meat then! You can't beat a good old free range cock."

"You and your cock."

"It still bloody works, you know."

"How would I?"

Leppo had spent months to track down Del Rafferty and was on the point of giving up when a contact in Edinburgh rang him and said he thought he may have seen Del in the city. "If it is him, at least he's out of my way for a while. I'll get him when he comes back down this way."

Chapter 34

Audrey was struggling.

A very large untidy man, who gave his surname merely as Smith had come to the reception area wanting to see the files for a planning application which impinged on his property. He felt he was being overlooked, and that he wasn't consulted about it, and it should have been dealt with properly and what are you going to do about it. All that sort of thing.

Audrey had seen that sort of thing before, but was struggling to get the detail of the property concerned from the man. He claimed that it was a private matter and he didn't want his private details spelt out in public.

"Would it help if we go into a quiet interview room, Mr Smith? Then we will be in a private space, and you can tell me where the property is," said Audrey, as calmly as she could.

"I don't know. You don't know about it, do you?"

"Well, until you tell me the detail of where it is, I can't find any files, or find out who dealt with the case in the first place, can I?" Audrey asked, and gradually led the man into the interview room, where he sat down and cried his eyes out.

"It's just not right, it's so unfair," he sobbed out the words, and Audrey thought it was time to get someone else to look after Mr Smith, and went and found the office first aider who came and managed to calm him down.

"Let's try again, then Mr Smith. Are you feeling up to telling me the story now?" asked Audrey, and Smith said that he wasn't Smith but he was Frank Crosby, and she managed to wheedle out of him that his house was in West Kenning.

"OK, that's good, Mr Crosby. Can you tell me when the building that you don't like was built?"

"Oh, I don't know, probably about three or four years ago."

"OK, can you tell me why you've come in today, then? Did you complain originally?"

"Course I did, but your young fella just told me not to worry about it, 'cos there weren't anything he could do."

"Right, now let's agree on a way forward shall we? I will try and find the file now, but only if you tell me your address, so that I can find the right one."

Crosby looked a bit vague as though he wasn't sure he should do this. After a minute or so, he told her and she told him to stay put, as she scampered back to her desk and asked Sandra to find out the history of planning applications on either side off his home.

Audrey breathed in deeply, drank some cold water and closed her eyes for a minute before popping out again to see if Frank was still there. He was, and she told him that she should have some information in ten minutes or so.

Sandra was trying to examine the digitised maps to track down the address that Frank had provided, as there were three streets with names that were not dissimilar, but she eventually found one that looked as though it might be the right place. She found some applications that had been dealt with five years earlier and tracked down the files on her computer. He had been right. He had written in at that point and argued against giving next door the permission.

The extension to Frank's next door property had been approved. There were notes from the case officer who had tested for sunlight and shadowing problems, and had then recommended approval. The recommendation was signed off by Jane.

Audrey went and told Frank that it was taking longer that she had hoped and it would not be much longer before she had an answer. She walked to Jane's office, knocked and was surprised to see that she was at her desk, as the digital diary shared by all the staff suggested she would be out.

"Glad you're in, Jane. It's a good while ago, but do you remember this one," and placed an extract from the file that she had printed off, in front of Jane, "only, the next door neighbour is in the interview room, having a bit of a moan."

"Oh, yes I do, funnily enough. There was a fair old kerfuffle at the time. It was before Clive's time here and I think Dave got caught up in the politics. Do you know what the old boy wants this time?"

"Not really, but he sort of said that he thought mistakes were made."

Jane was looking through the documents and asked, "Who dealt with it, then? Oh, yes, him."

"Who's "him"?" asked Audrey.

"Do you remember that dippy temp we had straight from Uni. It was him, I think. Maybe he did fail to pick up something. Ahhhh, but I signed it off. OK, Audrey, it might just clear the air if I go and see him"

They walked together to the room where Frank was still staring at the wall.

"Hello again, Frank," said Audrey, "This is Jane Seabrook, she is one of the senior staff here, and she will talk you through it, OK?"

Jane thanked Audrey as she left, and told Frank that she did remember the case as it had caused concern at the time. "Do tell me why it's taken you so long to come and talk about it again."

"Well, you see, it was a bit of a family dispute and my daughter's in-laws were behind the extension, and me and the missus didn't let on at the time."

"I see. Well I've looked at the file, and the lad who dealt with it isn't here anymore and the Chief at the time has retired. However, I must take a portion of the blame as I signed off the approval. So, I am very sorry indeed for whatever grief you went through at that time, and I hope you will take this apology with the sincerity it is meant."

Frank welled up. "Oh dear. Thank you for saying that, it has put my mind at rest. We've got used to the extension now, and the new neighbours are lovely."

"That's great Mr Crosby, all's well that ends well, eh?"

"Yes, you see the new neighbours are my grand-daughter and her man."

"How lovely for you," said Jane, welling up herself, "I wish you well. Goodbye, Mr Crosby."

"What a nice lady," thought Frank as he left to walk home.

JULY

Chapter 35

Jim Prentice was making good progress after much grieving over the loss of Hazel and had returned to work in the High School. The pupils were all delighted to see him back and gave him a huge round of applause at assembly. He was feeling more able to get on with his life and his teaching was fresh and enjoyable for his classes. He had asked his children to go to friends' homes after school, as he was going for a walk with Dave.

Throughout the late July afternoon and well into the evening the weather was warm and fresh when Dave picked Jim up from Swinton, and he drove south to park the car at the entrance to the Thompson Pingo trail. Jim knew about them as a geographic feature but had not seen the pingos and had never been on this walk. The pingos were dry as the weather had been hot, and there had been no rain for a fortnight, so the strange depressions in the meadows were a magnet for dragonflies and, unfortunately an awful lot of gnats which the pair of them swatted away with their arms.

During the walk they sat down on a bench and Dave took off his backpack and brought out a flask of icy water and a couple of small cups. He also extracted a hip flask and poured a couple of fingers of malt whisky and added a splash of icy water to each. "Just a splash," said Dave, adding, "I had an old Scottish golfing friend who only wanted his dram to be "just irritated" with water. "Good health, my friend," he said and noticed that Jim had a tear in his eye.

They went on their way without a further word until they reached a fence with a stile that led to the road back to the car, and they stopped for a breather. Dave asked, "How are the children coping, Jim?"

"I think they are doing alright now, thanks. Philly has really grown up in such a short space of time and has been a massive help in the house, and Zac has, I think, started to sort out his life. He has changed his group of friends and seems to be in with a good crowd. I'm so chuffed that he has started to get into rugby and the physical side of that will do him good."

"And what about yourself?"

"I think I'm on the up, thanks Dave, although I find myself feeling guilty that I didn't recognise what she had been feeling like before we got the diagnosis. At least I'm so glad we sorted out our wills a year ago. It felt too early to be doing that, but you never know what's round the corner, do you? I think I am ready for the next stage of my life now. I found out the other day that it had been possible for me to just go into a political hibernation for a short while, and I can go back to my role on the Council again. That will give me a focus."

"Delighted to hear it, Jim," said Dave, and patted him on the shoulder as they walked their way to the car for the ride home.

The police's investigation into the protests and damage at the poultry farm was under way and it was becoming clear that one of the organisations which was opposed to intensive farming had been involved, but they were struggling for evidence. It was eventually clarified that the on-site CCTV had been faulty, and that there had been no independent witnesses come forward.

Eventually a member of the public, who had passed by in his car realised that his dash-cam might have recorded some of the activity. He checked and converted the video onto his laptop and emailed it to the police.

Fortunately, the problem of the smell from the poultry production plant was quickly rectified after agreement with the Environmental Health Department, and no further complaints had been made.

Work was nearing completion in repairing the drainage at Christian Grimm's flats and an inspection from one of the building control officers was due. He had tried to do the work himself but chickened out when he got to the top of the ladder, so he pulled in a favour and got a local odd-jobber to carry out the work on the downpipe.

"Flipper" Francis came round at about four o'clock and looked at the work, and particularly at the joint where the pipe was discharging into the drain. "Flippin' heck,boy, what the hell is this?"

Christian tried to explain but had no idea what he was looking at. "I don't know," he said.

"I should think you don't, you flippin' need to get your man back and start again otherwise you are going to lose the flippin' wall. That water will go right under the foundations and wash the walls away."

With that, Flipper got in his car and drove back to the office. Whilst he was an old fashioned chap and thought you could "hang yourself with records", he decided that with in case he would record everything that he saw.

The fears that had previously gripped the nation over the reported virus were reducing gradually, but the prospect of another, or a resurrection of this year's one – if indeed there had been one – still hung over everyone, and as a result people were reluctant to make any changes to their lives, not least to the idea of moving house or investing in property. Therefore, sales and consequently prices of property plummeted. The owner of Len's preferred Maltings building was considering cancelling the contract, not least because no real progress had been made on the submission of a planning application, and so Len was given two weeks to sort out his side of things or remove himself from the acquisition.

Len was considering his options.

There was another great hoo-haa in the countryside.

The constantly increasing number of wind farms in the North Sea was causing trouble. Not that the wind farms themselves were the problem, but it was how to get the cables from them to the national grid. It seemed as though no one had thought of that at the time and now schemes were being publicised which involved ploughing great trenches through the countryside to get to the massive transformer stations.

Nature conservation organisations, lovers of the landscape and locals affected by the schemes were incensed.

So were the Vice-Admiral and the Lady wife. "Bloody vandals, I say," said Lady Hilda, "what say you, Douglas?"

"Good God, woman, we can't have these damn buggers

Destroying our British way of life. Bet it's Johnny Foreigner again.

"Those bloody Scandinavians invaded us long ago and now they want to destroy our land." Lady Hilda harrumphed "It's a disgrace, I shall write to Parliament."

(She said it as Paaah-lee-ah-mint).

"Good idea, old thing, he replied, "might be a load of bloody chineee money as well I don't doubt. Bastards, all of 'em."

Chapter 36

On the 30th of the month, the Public Inquiry into the refusal of the twenty two houses began in the Swinton village hall. A man in his late forties with a foppish hairstyle, the Inspector in charge of conducting the Inquiry was Robin Hird. He wore a dark suit with a blue striped shirt and a scarlet tie. With his files and his notebook open, he welcomed the public who were unaccustomed to such a formal occasion in the village, introduced himself and explained the procedures to be followed, and the detail of the application that was the subject to the appeal. He expected the appeal might last for two days, he would inspect the site at the conclusion of the hearing and would hope to make his decision within three months.

Robin Hird asked the District Council to put its case and Terry Whitefoot introduced himself as solicitor to the Council and Jason Quail who would give evidence, together with Frank Jones, an independent traffic engineer, and an consultant ecologist, Virginia Hickling.

Terry set out the brief detail of the case and then asked Jason to give his evidence to support the decision of the Council. Jason asked if his written statement could be taken as read, and that he would merely highlight the planning issues. He gave chapter and verse of Government advice, of County Council policy and a detail of the Council's Local Plan policies.

He explained that the site was not identified in any of these policy documents as being an appropriate place for development, that there was no evidence of a need for these proposals, there were road safety concerns, that the site was flooded earlier in the year, and that there were objections to the ecological impact the development would impose of the area.

At this point the public gallery applauded and cheered, and Mr Hird had to ask them to listen quietly to all that was given in evidence and not to be rowdy.

Paul Welham was supported by Bagley's barrister Mr Adam McCann QC who rose and addressed Jason. "How long have you been a planning officer with the Council, Mr Quail?"

"I've been here nearly four years, Sir."

"You say you are a member of the Royal Town Planning Institute. What grade of membership do you hold?"

"I am a Licentiate Member."

"So, you are not a fully qualified Chartered Town Planner."

Jason looked coolly at McCann.

"Mr Quail?"

"Yes?"

"You are not a fully qualified Chartered Town Planner."

"I'm sorry, is that a question?"

"It is."

"You are correct."

"So, how are we to believe that you are sufficiently expert to give evidence on behalf of the Council, Mr Quail?"

"Believe what you wish, Sir. I know the policies that are relevant in this case and I know the issues that are relevant too. I hope the Inspector will respect that."

Terry was feeling a bit uncomfortable at this exchange and wanted to stand to defend Jason when Robin Hird intervened and asked McCann if he had any questions that were pertinent to the case. Adam McCann asked, "This version of the Local Plan was approved four years ago. Am I right?"

"Yes"

"So it is out of date, yes?"

"It is the current Plan with the current set of policies, and in accordance with national and local requirements is in the process of being reviewed."

"So, the review might conclude that the site is acceptable for this proposal. Do you agree?"

"I agree that there is a review under way, and I cannot second guess what it will say."

"That implies that the site may be appropriate. I suggest that that your out of date Plan is quite useless in the circumstances."

"The law, and I suspect you know this, requires applications to be judged on current policies, and as the Inspector will know, that is what has been the case here."

With that McCann sat down and Jason breathed a sigh of relief.

Mr Hird said that he had no points of clarification for Jason, and suggested they break for lunch, to which the gallery ignored the previous request and gave another round of applause.

Jason and Terry went to the village pub for lunch, and so did the Inspector. They nodded to each other and distanced themselves so that they would not be seen to be influencing him.

When the Inquiry resumed in the afternoon, Adam McCann apologised to the Inspector and indicated that he had a severe migraine and asked that the afternoon session be postponed.

Terry agreed and with much reluctance Robin Hird agreed and asked that the Inquiry should be reconvened at 9.30 the following day.

On the chance that there may be a third day required Terry asked Jerry Hollis, the Clerk to the Parish Council, if the hall could be reserved for that day as well.

It meant that the tap-dance and synchronised baton twirling classes would have to be cancelled.

The following morning, on the dot of nine thirty, Robin Hird announced the reconvening of the formalities, and asked Terry to continue the Council's case.

Terry welcomed back the appellant's barrister, and hoped he had recovered. He then asked the County Council's transport officer to amplify his written statement. Frank Jones said that the visibility splays were not adequate and it was clear that to make them so would involve the acquisition of additional land. The road network in the area was tortuous and there had been a number of accidents in the last three years. Further development here would add to waiting times at a number of junctions in the town.

Adam McCann asked Frank, "Mr Jones, please describe the types of accident that have taken place over the last three years, and how many fatalities these involved."

"There was an accident where two cars brushed against each other damaging the sides and wing mirrors of the cars. One car collided with a telegraph pole, one cyclist was forced into a ditch by a car which was trying to avoid another one going in the opposite direction, and one where a skip lorry damaged a tractor. There have not been any fatalities in these cases."

"Thank you. So, four notified accidents in three years with no fatalities! Hardly a major blackspot, then." "Now, did you advise my client about the inadequate visibility splays?"

"The advice in the Council's design handbook makes the requirement very clear."

"I repeat, was my client advised of this?"

"Your client was advised by professional experts who would understand these things."

"So, the matter was not referred to in any discussion or correspondence."

"Not as far as I am aware, but if your client's agents had been in touch with my colleagues, I would have expected the issue to have been raised."

"But you don't know this?"

"No."

"Mr Jones, is it true that some roads and some roundabouts designed by your Council or designed by consultants, and approved and implemented by the County Council have had to be redesigned some months after construction?"

"I'm not sure the relevance of that."

"Are you not? I suggest it shows that the judgement of your highways department is very suspect."

"Now, let us move onto your other point. You say that the proposed development would increase waiting times at junctions in the town. How would you know where the residents would want to go?"

"Our modelling of the current situation has been used to consider what problems the extra traffic would create."

"Do you know how many extra vehicles would be generated by this development?"

"Not exactly, but we have averages for estates of this type."

"So an average will come from low numbers to higher ones. Is that right?"

"Yes."

"So it is possible that there might be very few vehicles here. People will be satisfied to use local shops, do their grocery shopping online as well as any for major articles for the house and garden, and, Mr Jones, there is an excellent bus service through the village. Am I right?"

"It is possible, but highly unlikely."

McCann turned to the Inspector. "So, Sir, we have evidence that shows the number of accidents along the road to the village is minimal, with no fatalities. We have a highway authority that is justifiably criticised, and no clear evidence of any road safety danger. I suggest there are no justifiable highway objections to the proposal."

Frank Jones sat quietly and wondered if he had been right.

Next up was Virginia Hickling, an ecologist who gave a short address indicating that there would be a loss of wildflowers from the meadow and the consequent effect on wildlife, and that no suitable replacement habitat had been offered in the application. She indicated the types of insects, for example bees, butterflies and moths that would feed on the wildflowers and how the plants in the winter would protect hibernating fauna.

"Ms Hickling, have you surveyed the site to confirm and substantiate your assertions?" asked McCann.

"Yes, I have."

"And are you convinced that the generalised nature of your objection is sufficient to warrant this appeal being dismissed?"

"I am indeed."

"We will see what our expert has to say, then Ms Hickling."

With that he sat down

Robin Hird, thanked the witnesses for their time and clarity in their responses, and closed the session for lunch to be taken.

After lunch, Adam McCann opened proceedings by emphasising that the Council's policy was out of date and that the need for housing was greater than ever. More people were choosing to live single lives, and there was an increase in families splitting up. Many folk also have a desire to improve their living conditions by preferring a life in the countryside. The site was on the edge of an existing village and not out in the open. There was no threat to public safety on the roads and that the threat to wildlife was not an overriding factor. He asked Paul Welham to present his case.

As ever, Paul was full of confidence and wanted to read the whole of his evidence "so that there was no chance of misunderstanding anything" and took half an hour to do so.

Jason was growing irritated and so were some in the public gallery. At one point a member of the public said, "that is a lie. He can't say that without being challenged."

The Inspector was in control. "Sir, please allow all the witnesses to give their evidence. There will be a chance for each witness to be questioned both by the Council, and by me, and of course, there are others who have asked to present their views who will get a chance to argue whichever way they choose. I do insist that we should not have outbursts from anyone during witnesses' evidence. Thank you. Please proceed, Mr Welham."

Paul had emphasised the lack of opportunity for new people to enjoy a life in the village, the fact that the Local Plan was so out of date that it no longer complied with Government targets, and that the infrastructure within the village made it suitable for development.

Terry Whitefoot rose to question Paul.

"Mr Welham, the fact that there is demand for more housing is not the point here, but where it should be located. Why did your client choose Swinton?"

"Because it has excellent facilities and can cope with further development. It has a thriving school with places available, the shops are successful and there is a good bus service. It meets all the necessary requirements."

"And, given that the village might be appropriate to accept more houses, how many other sites did you explore?"

"Three or four."

"Is it three or is it four?"

"I think it was three."

"So, not four, then. Would you show us which sites you did examine."

Paul was shuffling in his seat and through his papers. "I don't have those marked on a plan."

"Very well, Mr Welham, so if I were to give you a map of the village, would you point these out, please?" Terry asked Jason for a map of the parish and passed it to Paul. "Please indicate the sites with a red mark."

Paul hesitated, racked his brains for a suitable response and said, "I don't think that is appropriate as there is commercially confidential information at stake and it might compromise our position."

"That is nonsense, Mr Welham. You have chosen to demand a Public Inquiry into this case and you are refusing to be open and honest with a vital piece of information. How can the Inspector possibly be able to judge the application if alternative sites have not been examined? I suggest that you did not look at any other sites. Am I right?"

"It is difficult to "

"Am I right?" Terry was at his best at this point, and was enjoying himself.

So was Jason, who was glad that Terry was on his side.

Paul was losing the early bravado and replied, meekly, "Er, yes."

"I am struggling, now, Mr Welham, in that you have just lied to the Inquiry and I am in a quandary to know which parts of your testimony I can trust. I think the Inspector will feel the same. So can we continue on the understanding that this was the only site chosen? Why was that?"

"I was not a party to that decision, so I can't help you with that."

"Was it down to the ownership of the site, the price, or what?"

"I don't know."

"Your client is called Bagleys. They are not a well known company. Who are the company directors, please?"

"It is a company from Lincolnshire."

"Answer the question, please."

"It is a private family firm."

"Please, Mr Welham, please answer my question."

"I think they are Patrick and Melissa Bagley."

"Thank you. What is their main business then, as I assume it is not residential development?"

"They are farmers."

"You state in your application documents that the owners of the site are the Trustees of Mrs Elsie Bryant. Is there any relationship between the trustees and Mr & Mrs Bagley?"

"I have not been told anything about that."

"Would it surprise you to know that our investigations indicate that Mr & Mrs Bagley are the only trustees and that Mrs Elsie Bryant was their great aunt?"

"I had no idea, and frankly my job was to help prepare and submit the application."

Terry continued to question Paul for another quarter of an hour and he decided to finish with a question that had nothing to do with the appeal. "Is it true, Mr Welham that Mrs Bagley is your sister?"

After what seemed like a very long pause, Paul said, "yes, she is."

Terry sat down.

There were astonished cries from the public gallery and someone said "Well, now we know what they were up to!"

Robin Hird decided that the heat of the day and the lack of any air conditioning was making the continuation of the session undesirable for him, for the participants as well as the folk in the public gallery, and announced that the session was closed and that the Inquiry would resume at nine thirty in the morning.

Jason went home is high spirits. He had thanked Terry for his help and support and said he loved the way he teased the real reason for wanting the approval out of Paul Welham.

He had a couple of pints in the pub, grabbed some food, changed and went back to the pub.

Chapter 37

As promised, Jane met up with Jim and they decided to go for a walk before going for a drink and something to eat. He picked her up at seven o'clock and they walked the lanes on the edge of the town before they drove out to one of the nearby country pubs. Jim was being careful as he had to drive home so just had a half of shandy, whereas Jane had a glass of Chablis. She ordered a shellfish salad and Jim went for the venison steak, and they chatted about the weather, their children and the pressures at work. Jane ordered another glass of the excellent wine. The food was good and plentiful, so they passed on a sweet and sat and drank a weak cup of coffee with mints.

They got into Jim's Subaru and he drove back to Jane's house where she asked if he fancied a better cup of coffee. In they went and the coffee machine was soon doing its work. Jim was looking through the collection of books, music and the local watercolours when he was surprised to find that she had crept up behind him and wrapped her arms around him. He turned and she pushed her face up to his and kissed him firmly on the lips.

They fell together onto the sofa, and held each other for what seemed ages. Eventually, Jane whispered in his ear, "Oh Jim, I have been wanting this for ages, but I could not force myself into your time of grief."

"Jane, you know what I have felt for you and I have felt so guilty with Hazel so ill, but now?"

"Do you want to go upstairs?" she asked, and without waiting for an answer she led him by the hand and up the stairs to her bedroom.

She undressed to her full nakedness and looked at Jim, who was not rushing. He was taking in the sheer beauty of her body, the length of her hair, the firmness and smoothness of her breasts, the tautness of her stomach, the length of her slim legs, and the beauty between them. He took his clothes off and slipped under the cool sheet and wrapped his arms around her and wept like a child.

"I have felt so lonely," he said, "so wretched and so afraid. I had no idea I could ever feel passion again."

"Oh you can, Jim, you will feel the passion, and ...... feel mine. Please."

"After the last six months, I'm not sure that I can."

"Oh you can, Jim, you can."

He did.

Christian Grimm was playing golf at the West Kenning Golf and Country Club on a bright sunny Sunday morning when amidst the banter someone spotted a plume of black smoke rising from what appeared to be the centre of town.

"Good old fire going on down there. It might be someone getting their own back on Len!" he said, and the other three fell about laughing.

Christian played rather well after that and enjoyed his pint and whisky chaser in the bar with his playing partners, swapping golfing stories of past times.

He drove home to find a police car and two fire engines at his house and crowds of onlookers looking either frightened or, surprisingly, smiling.

Christian feared for his two cats, until he realised that the fire was in the large storage shed to the rear of the property. It was destroyed.

Nothing left except a bicycle frame, some metal springs from an old sofa and the frame of an old metal bedstead.

This was where he stored the furniture for his flats, present and future. He had bought most of it at local auctions for a knock down price, thinking that many were of antique vintage.

He had recorded them in an inventory of sorts, and had added that list to his house insurance.

The following day he rang the insurance company who asked a series of questions in order to ascertain whose property was destroyed. He was asked who else lived in the large house and he said that he was helping out Jose Viana, a Portuguese worker in the town and that Jose had owned some of the furniture but it was all listed on his inventory.

The insurers said that they would investigate and let him know in a few days.

In Hayle, the villagers were getting organised against Davie McDonald's proposal to demolish the pub and build seven houses on the site.

They had made contact with Raj Hossein, the planning officer dealing with the case, who was trying to make some sort of sense of the economics and the viability of the pub.

From the village, Nick Beckham was charged with getting to grips with the numbers, and made contact with their friends, the previous owners, to see if they would allow the use of their annual figures.

As they had expected, it was quite clear that it wasn't the pub that was at fault in creating a non-viable financial concern, but the owners, landlords or whoever was making the decisions to try and make the business work.

Nick got a peek at the previous owners' business plans and company accounts, and noted down the relevant information.

He would talk to Raj.

AUGUST

Chapter 38

The first of the month saw the third day of the planning appeal's inquiry and Robin Hird asked that all parties should try and be as efficient as they could to ensure the proceedings were completed as soon as possible.

Adam McCann called his traffic expert, Alex Murphy. In the interests of timeliness Alex asked if his written statement might be taken as read, and the inspector and Terry Whitefoot agreed subject to him giving a brief summary of his evidence so that the public could understand his arguments. He reiterated McCann's opening statement arguing that the road network was perfectly capable of taking the extra traffic and that there was no risk to traffic safety.

Terry rose to question him. "Mr Murphy, good day to you. The proposal is for twenty two homes. Have you counted the number of bedrooms in the proposal?"

"No I haven't."

"Then would you please examine the plans closely and let me know the number you come up with?"

After a few minutes he replied, "I make it seventy seven."

"Please explain your calculation."

"Two bungalows with two bedrooms, seven houses with three bedrooms and thirteen houses with four."

"I agree, thank you."

Terry continued, "So whilst it is unlikely, it is not impossible for the dwellings to be homes to families with every bedroom used by someone over seventeen, and on that basis there might be seventy seven cars and not to say work vans as well, together with visitors' cars. Unlikely but it is possible. Will you agree?"

"Highly unlikely."

"But it is possible. Worst case, Yes?"

"Yes, definitely worst case."

"And, so, are you really saying that this amount of traffic will not have an adverse effect on the road network?

"Even if that was the case, I believe I am right."

"OK, thank you. That will be all. Oh, sorry, just for clarification, are you related to the applicants?"

"No I am not."

Giggles in the public gallery, and even Robin Hird allowed himself a smile.

Adam McCann said that their ecologist had called in sick, but had previously submitted her statement of evidence, and asked that this may be recorded as the case for the appellants, and this was agreed.

Robin asked if members of the public who had asked to be heard were present, and still wished to put their views to the Inquiry. Elizabeth Kaye, the Parish Council Chairman raised her hand and gave her name, as did local shopkeeper Simon Cleverley and Father Bertie Halman a friar from the friary a couple of miles from the site. Elizabeth asked if she might be last in the list.

Simon Cleverley said that he had lived in the village for the last five years and that the general stores that he kept with his wife had done reasonably well over time, but had struggled recently with an increased use of online grocery shopping, so a number of new customers coming to visit them in the village would be welcome to him and the other commercial businesses there.

Terry asked him if he thought that the new residents were just as likely as the existing to do their grocery shopping online, and Simon agreed that he didn't see why not.

Father Bertie Halman spoke briefly to explain that the friary overlooked the site and would intrude into the peaceful view of the valley, and that the noise from the construction site would not be welcome either.

And so to Elizabeth who put the view of the Parish Council. She was clear and assertive, stating that the Parish was in unanimous opposition to the scheme. Housing of this scale was not required in the village, that the site was not appropriate, and that there were, despite what the appellants said, real concerns about the likely increase in traffic. She understood the views of commercial interests but they were not of sufficient strength to overturn the Parish view.

Terry was asked if he wished to sum up the Council's case, and indeed he did.

"Sir, whilst not a planning reason, it is clear that the application was submitted in order to satisfy family greed. The proposal had no merit whatsoever. It had been promulgated by a witness who lied to us all, and more importantly, to you. Its details are born of no local investigations, it will increase the amount of traffic in rural lanes, the site floods and there are ecological concerns. It is a thoroughly bad proposal and, Sir, the appeal should be dismissed Also, if I may, Sir, the Council wishes to make an application for costs on the basis of the deception that has been seen so clearly these past three days.

Adam McCann concluded the formal part of the process with a weak speech that barely touched any merits of the case and asked for the appeal to succeed.

Robin Hird then closed the session, thanked the public for attending, and the participants, and announced that he would visit the site immediately for any of the parties to point out any features that needed clarifying. He would then present his report to the Secretary of State for confirmation of his decision within a couple of months.

Chapter 39

Jim was so much happier, and with the school holidays in full swing he asked Zac and Philippa what they wanted to do. Did they want a week in the sun – not that it wasn't sunny in Swinton, - or a trip to the hills for a walking holiday? Philippa wanted to go abroad, Zac wasn't particularly bothered, but agreed to go and so Jim got them to go to Catalonia. There they were close to the beach, could have a day walking in the hills, have a day in Barcelona or check out the Dali museum in Figueres. It was a good family week and they caught the sun, although Jim's mind was always with Jane.

Jane had taken the same week to take the girls to see her mum and dad in Nottingham, but it was clear after a few days that they were bored stiff and wanted to get back home and to the riding school. Nothing that Jane suggested for them to do was of the slightest interest. She too was lusting after more time with Jim and couldn't wait to get home.

As soon as they got back, she was on the phone to the CSA to see what progress had been made in the action to get more money out of John. She fumed when she was told that they couldn't get hold of him and his firm told them that he was away for three weeks. Mexico they thought, but weren't sure.

"Bastard, bastard, bastard. He can do that, but he can't do right by his children," she ranted to no one but herself.

Jason Quail, had taken the bull by the horns and asked Sandra from the office if she wanted a week hiking in the

Lake District. He was pleasantly surprised when she said she was up for it, and so he had booked a cabin in the Langdale Valley. They made the trip in five hours, found their home for the week and then went to the Britannia at Elterwater for a few pints and a plate of great food.

Sandra was as fit as a flea and was used to the hills, having been taken there many times by her mum and dad when she was in her mid-teens. They had bedded down in separate rooms and next day had a full breakfast thanks to Sandra's cooking. They packed some sandwiches and decided to have a gentle first day's walk to the top of the valley where the road turns south, and where straight on is the track leading to the climb towards Bowmore. Partway up the slopes it became clear that the weather was going to close in, so they turned round and strode back to base.

The next day they thought they would give a try climbing from Grasmere to Easdale Tarn and across the ridges to the Langdale Pikes. This would test their fitness and endurance. The plan was to descend to the pub at the base of the Pikes and walk back home, but also in the hope that the bus may come along at the right time. They made it, and, totally shattered, they flopped down on the sofa for an evening of television, and were asleep within minutes.

Three more days of walking the fells and they knew they had reached the end of their endurance, and on the last evening felt that they had known each other so well that they fell into each other's arms and enjoyed their bodies to the point of real exhaustion.

It had been a great week.

The Vice-Admiral had decided to take the Lady Hilda on a cruise into the Mediterranean, and rather than fly south to catch the ship, he decided to travel to Southampton and embark there. The traffic on the way was horrendous with roadworks on the motorways and a couple of accidents en route.

Hilda was reading her book as they drove, but paused to say, "Bit of a bugger, these delays, eh, Douglas?"

"Too bloody right. I thought this was the best way, but I'm starting to regret it now. Bloody frustrating way to start a holiday."

"I know dear, but just take the patience pills!"

It took them two hours longer that he had planned but they arrived in time to park the Bentley and be shown to their cabin. They dumped their luggage on the bed and went to the bar for an early "snifter" or three, just to rid themselves of the angst of the journey.

Back in their cabin, they unpacked their cases, showered and dressed for dinner.

"Smart casual tonight, I think Hilda. We can leave the posh stuff for another night. I brought the medals in case we get invited to sit with the Captain."

Apart from the effects of the swell around the Bay of Biscay, when Hilda was very quiet, they had a relaxing week, enjoyed the sights. They had met some "really sweet people" according to Hilda, whereas her husband thought they were a bunch of "drippy wets and socialists".

Well fed and watered, they said their "au revoirs" and had a better journey home.

Clive Painter took himself away for a week walking in the Peak District and the Yorkshire Dales. He had booked himself into a pub near Edale and had found company there for a chat and a meal before a couple of days on the hills and up to Kinder Scout. He then moved into Wensleydale for some gentle hiking with his camera at the ready. The weather was kind to him with quiet southerly breezes just taking off a bit of the heat of the sun.

A good week, good food, good beer, and all to unwind and get back to nature.

Len was still trying to find someone to help him put together his planning application. In conjunction with the Town Council he had managed to put forward a proposal for a charitable trust to front the application, but that was taking ages to be registered, and some very awkward questions were being asked.

Chapter 40

Dave Wakefield had chatted with Michelle and they had decided not to holiday in August and he had spent more time talking to Tony Chaplin at the Council, and carrying out his own research into the Green Energy project. He was getting a clearer insight into what was required in terms of size and location of the site, in order for the proposal to stand a reasonable chance of success. From all his experience, he knew that it would be essential to take the local residents along with the idea, as he was sure that mass objections would probably scupper the scheme, and probably frighten off the people behind it.

He needed to make sure that his landowner contact had a site that ticked all the right boxes.

The ideal location was close to a main road, sheltered from view, sufficiently away from any houses and with easy access to the farming community.

Maybe in the Forest? Did it have to be in Parston District? He decided to take Michelle out for a drive one day to look at a series of possibilities, some of which he had in mind from those he had dealt with in the past.

If he found the right site, he would take Tony Chaplin and a highways officer to look at it. Then, of course, was the matter of whether or not the landowner could be persuaded to get involved.

Plenty to think about, plenty to work on. It would keep his mind active for a month or three.

In the village of Hayle, the residents had formed a formal group to see if the purchase of the pub as a cooperative venture would be possible. Nick Beckham was still playing with figures, and it looked as though the site value, as currently proposed by Davie McDonald, would be beyond their reach. It was therefore imperative to keep the pub and its land as one entity and put a value on it in its existing state. It was vital then, that the planning proposal be refused. They had also asked the Council to designate it a "Community Asset".

Obviously Davie was opposed to this and argued that if no-one used the pub, it could hardly be an asset to the community. Nick argued that the pub itself was an asset and certainly had been well used by the community in the recent past, before Davie bought it.

Geoff Pulling was preparing a way to celebrate his first year in real journalism, and was gathering a list of the issues that had been raised and reported by him. He was surprised that they included the most mundane birthday celebrations of a lady in one of the Care Homes who had celebrated her one hundredth birthday, although, poor soul, she was in such an awful state that he doubted if she had any idea about what was going on. Still he had reflected that it might have been his great-Nan, and he was thankful that she had passed away quietly and peacefully a couple of years ago. There were also a few reports of the local football and cricket teams, a number of funerals, some Parish Council meetings and the general chaos at the District Council.

It had been enjoyably varied.

Christian Grimm, who was basically idle by nature, was getting really frustrated. There had been a lack of communication from his insurance company relating to his claim for the loss of his property in the fire. The last time he had chased them, they asked for detailed receipts for the items lost, so that values could be established. Needless to say, as he had bought them in second hand shops and auctions, and paid by cash, the number of receipts was minimal. In fact, non-existent.

He had blamed the Portuguese guy living in the house with him for losing the documents when he was cleaning the part of the house that Christian loosely described as "his office". In reality, this was the corner of a spare bedroom that stored boxes of files that he hadn't looked at for twenty years, a suitcase full of old clothes that he couldn't get into, but thought that with a bit of slimming he would use again and a large trunk full of "collectables" that he thought would, one day, make him a fortune.

Without the receipts he was in a muddle, and so he rang the insurers again to try and speak to a more accommodating person. In doing so, he put on an unusual accent that partly mimicked the Portuguese lad, but this brought little joy, as the same woman answered the phone, and recognised his voice. "Good afternoon, Mr Grimm. Now I know you are claiming that some of the items were valuable antiques, but there is no evidence of this. There are no photographs, no receipts and the loss adjuster only saw metal remains of a bicycle, a bed, and a couple of unidentifiable items. Now, we can see that the building needs replacing, although your policy was on a "like for like" basis and not new for old". We accept, from the amount of charred remains, that there were many items within the building. But we don't know what."

"But I gave you an inventory of the contents."

"Yes, but it was just a list. No pictures, no valuations, and, to be frank, nothing we can use as evidence. I can make you an offer for the replacement shed and a nominal figure for the contents."

"You better send that then," said a downcast Grimm. He put the phone down and opened a bottle of Shiraz.

This was just the start of his worries as he had been notified that he was to appear before the Magistrate's Court in relation to his failure to produce sound, safe and healthy housing conditions for his tenants.

Towards the end of the month, back in the planning office, work was under way to prepare final reports to the Planning Committee in September. Clive had asked that the team work on these concerning the Local Plan progress, the conclusion of the Historic Buildings at Risk and the issue of fly posting.

Paul and Andrea were still without the final details they were hoping for to be able to analyse the real needs for housing and they therefore had to make the matter more generalised, and had come to the conclusion that adding to towns was still the preferred way of allowing for expansion.

Jane and "Jimmy" Young were still scratching their heads as to how best to deal with the fly posting issue but had decided to set out all the problems and solutions for the Committee to decide, and Clive was happy with that approach.

HB's report was detailed and clear. Amongst that list was the ammunition store in Dilford, a church with a failing roof and the two malting buildings in West Kenning.

Back in March, the committee had asked for clarity on the action that could, or should be taken against owners of these buildings. The report suggested that there were formal procedures which were available, but that the Council had always taken an approach of trying to encourage and persuade owners to do the right thing. Failing that the Council might step in and take a charge on the property, carry out the work and try and obtain the money from the owner. This was often easier said than done; it was very time consuming, and with the limited resources at their disposal, was usually discounted.

The continued existence of the buildings in the list was proof of the ineffectiveness of this approach.

The further development of West Kenning was reliant on improvements to the sewerage system throughout the town It had long been clear that some major new engineering projects were required. One of these ran close to some old buildings and the engineers were therefore, having to be particularly careful.

Suddenly there was a massive explosion which was heard throughout the town and over ten miles away. Fire sirens, police, ambulance were all called and the public were kept well away from the danger. It transpired that a JCB was digging the trench for the pipe-work when it hit an unreported or previously surveyed bomb from World War II. The old buildings near the centre of town had windows and walls blown apart, and the real concern was for the nearby historic malting building.

Everyone assumed that this was Len's baby and some were even cruel enough to say that he set the bomb off to claim insurance money. In truth, this was not that building, but the one used by the drug dealers. There had been no chance for the JCB driver to survive and three other site workers were badly injured.

When the emergency services had cleared the area and dealt with the injured and shocked, they went, carefully inside the building and to their utter horror saw the dead bodies of three teenagers, and a big black adult.

Leppo.

Avril had been one of the first to the scene, and wrote:-

> **Tragedy in town. Four killed in bomb explosion.**
>
> *In a devastating accident, West Kenning experienced a tragedy for construction workers, destruction of ancient buildings and an occurrence that will be remembered for many a day. An undetected wartime bomb which had fallen some eighty years ago was struck by machinery excavating a channel for the town's improved sewers. The driver was killed and many others injured. The extraordinary power of the bomb wrecked part of the adjacent old maltings building and we regret to say that three young men from the town and from nearby villages who were in that*

building were discovered, killed by falling masonry or cut to ribbons by flying shards of cast iron.

That building had been used as a shelter for homeless people and for trading and taking of drugs. Some will feel sorry for the plight of young people who were in the depths of despair but when you know that also killed was a London based drug dealer you may feel that some good has come from such tragedy.

EPILOGUE

Many months later, Jane got a result from the CSA, and as she expected, her salary had been taken into account, but after settling the matter without having to go to a Court hearing, John had to pay an extra four hundred pounds a month, backdated nine months.

She and Jim got themselves together more often, and the arrangement was encouraged and enjoyed by all the children.

Zac seemed to get his life back on an even keel, and over the months and after a fair number of lessons he managed to pass his driving test. He was saving up for his first car, and Jim had promised him some help with that once he got himself into work.

He started that phase of his life with an apprenticeship at a large firm of architects in Norwich, and was doing well, and was certainly popular with the staff.

Dave's investigations into the Green Energy Park took months to resolve, and it proved impossible to find a site which met all the technical criteria as well as being acceptable to the local residents. The investors behind the idea ran out of patience and another great idea in principle was quashed. Similar to what had happened some years earlier regarding waste incinerators.

Christian was reaching a crossroads. He was still waiting for his court case to come up, and was fearing a criminal record that would affect his financing arrangements, so he decided to try and sort his business life out by selling two of his buildings that each housed four flats. From the proceeds he made enough from those sales to put the remaining three into decent shape.

He re-housed Jordan and Emily, and gave them a two month rent-free period as a gesture of goodwill. Local people were both pleased and astonished.

Geoff wrote:-

Lesson learnt

It is with much pleasure that we can write a really joyful column congratulating Mr Christian Grimm on the way he has changed his attitude towards the responsibilities he holds towards his tenants. By restructuring his business he has funded quality renovations of three buildings, including the flat of Jordan Brooks and Emily Rizzo.

We praise the young couple for raising the matter, and are pleased that our campaign has paid off.

The tragedy that killed local boys as well as Leppo, created such a storm that efforts to give help to the addicts were tripled. Many were in treatment and the town felt more clean and healthy.

At least for a while.

The residents in the village of Hayle were supported by a local brewery and by a successful crowd-funding venture, and eventually bought the Golden Horseshoe and got on with the process of refurbishment and the employment of a chef. After a further year, the profits were rolling in and the community had the venue that it wanted and needed.

Jason was over the moon to learn that the appeal for the site in Swinton had been dismissed, and the costs application against the Bagleys had been approved. He had told Jim and they had enjoyed a celebratory pint with Jane.

The Vice-Admiral and Lady Hilda were pleased to read of this in the Broad Norfolk Post. He said, "I say, Hilda, those buggers who wanted to build those little boxes in Swinton have got their comeuppance. Bloody good job too, what?"

"I know, dear. I suspect there will be a few glasses of bubbly spilt over there!"

"I reckon we should do the same!"

Len's suspension was over and he returned to his work with the Council, albeit on the back benches until the deferred election in the following May. The notion of joint working was being held in high regard but the majority of the electorate had little interest and voted along their traditional lines, and the Conservatives won a clear majority.

Craig set about reorganising his top team of Chairmen, and having to fill the positions that had been held by Tom and Fiona. He went out of his way to pay tribute to them for their cooperative approach and their exceptional work. Fiona was particularly upset, but put her enthusiasm into pushing for green energy projects. She spoke with Tony Chaplin and with Dave, and promised to put her support behind the right site – if they ever found it.

Len had put himself up for re-election, and gained a resounding victory from local voters, for he was seen, despite all his faults, as someone who fought for his town, had some good ideas but went about it the wrong way.

Eventually his efforts to get his development project fell flat. The owners of that set of malting buildings, being aware of the continued fall in property prices wanted to get something out of the site and managed to find a buyer.

Within a year Len had keeled over and died, just a few weeks after Cass had passed away.

The buildings were bought by a local Housing Association which developed them into flats with a community meeting room.

It was called Pollox Hall.

The locals called it something else.